FIND ME

Nell Grey

CONTENTS

PROLOGUE

--------*--------

Slamming the sizzling pizza onto the worktop Sion Edwards made a lunge for the ringing house phone, grabbing it just before it clicked to the answer machine.

"Hey, Jac! How ya doin'?"

He felt with his fingers for the wheeled cutter in the drawer as he held the phone to his ear. It was hard to hear his housemate above the noise of the bar.

"Sorry, mate. I'm not sure I'm gonna make it for the pool game. I've not long got back. I need a shower and I haven't eaten yet… I can't hear ya, pal? What did you say? Claire's working tonight? …Oh, okay, I'll see how I feel. I *might* come out later on… See ya."

He placed the receiver back into the cradle, thinking about Claire and how he was going to get her to go out with him. Wondering how many people still used landlines except in these rural parts. Not that he was grumbling. This remote corner of Wales with its green mountains sweeping into the Irish Sea, it wasn't a bad place to be holed up.

The pizza's doughy base steamed as he rolled through the molten cheese and the delicious grease-laden pepperoni rounds. Not the healthiest of choices but after six hours of climbing his body was craving carbs.

Today, he'd finally ticked off the big one. The Dervish Slab was every climber's ultimate challenge. And Sion had picked his route carefully, moving fluidly up the sheer quarry wall, keeping momentum. Except for once. And in that once, his heart had lurched in sheer terror as the slate crumbled away in his fingertips. Grip gone, his toes slipped. A millisecond. It was all it had taken for the ground to come up dizzyingly close as he plunged towards his death.

The area around his ribs was still sore from where he'd jolted to a stop. Thankfully, the iron piton had held firm and he'd found himself dangling in mid-air. Light-headed. Blood and adrenaline pumping furiously, hanging onto life at the end of a rope.

It had been a close one.

Sion took another burning bite.

What was that?

He bristled.

Straining his ears he listened again.

The noise was faint but unexpected all the same.

A little louder now.

The unmistakable hum of a car engine. And a crunching sound too. Tyres on gravel as it neared the cottage.

Had something happened?

His special forces training kicked in like muscle memory. The pizza lay forgotten as Sion automatically plunged himself into darkness.

A split-second later car headlights began pooling onto the window of the kitchen door.

Was it the Scousers? Had they found out?

He willed that from his mind. None of those mad mongrels would ever find him out here.

Who was it, then? Jac's remote cottage never had social callers.

Keeping low, he stalked up the stairs and into the bedroom for his kit bag and the semi-automatic rifle.

Armed, he crept back down to the kitchen window. Staying in the shadows by the wall he clicked the safety catch and lifted the gun ready to fire.

Using the tip of the barrel he widened the gap in the blinds, then lined up the stationary SUV in the sight. Tracking the shadow of the driver's head as the door opened, his finger lay poised on the trigger ready to squeeze as they stepped out.

Maureen.

His shoulders slumped, and blowing out a deep breath he dropped the gun and clicked the safety back on.

What was she doing here at this time?

Bounding up the stairs he stashed the gun and returned, flicking the lights on and opening the kitchen door just as her finger pressed the bell.

He tried to look calm even though he didn't feel it.

His neighbour stood before him; shrunken, grey-haired and dishevelled in the headlights of the truck. The engine was still running.

"Are you alright?"

Pale and hollow-eyed, it was obvious she wasn't.

"What's happened?"

"I... I killed him."

What? Had he heard her right?

It seemed he had.

She looked like she was in shock.

Sion cleared his throat.

"Show me."

Sion drove her the half-mile back to the farmhouse. Her jaw set firm. Her mouth clamped shut. He hoped it wouldn't be too gruesome. There was no blood on her.

Everyone knew that Maureen's husband was an alcoholic. It was how Jac had got to rent the land and the farm cottage when he came out of the army. Glyn wasn't coping. And from what Sion had witnessed, he was a mean bastard too.

And now Glyn Evans was lying before him, rolled into the recovery position on the kitchen floor.

Holding up his wrist, Sion prayed for a pulse. But the old farmer was gone.

Maureen, a retired nurse knew that already.

Picking the syringe up off the floor, Sion automatically rinsed and pocketed it, together with the empty vials lying discarded on the worktop. He'd dispose of those another time, somewhere far from here.

What was he playing at?

This was a crime scene. And from what he could see, Maureen had killed her husband with a lethal dose of insulin. Even with a defence of diminished responsibility, she was still facing time in jail. Time they both knew Maureen didn't have.

"He was gonna use the kettle on me."

Maureen's words punctured the silence.

"He's done it to me once before, you know?"

Her eyes met Sion's.

"Scalded me all down my shoulder."

"Where did you inject him?"

"Over there."

She pointed towards the kettle still sitting on its base on the worktop.

She was in shock. It wasn't what he meant but he let her carry on.

"He came raging into the kitchen when I was making a cuppa. And he'd got that mad look on him. When he gets like that, it usually terrifies me. This time though, I'm not sure why, but something inside me flipped. He made me so *bloody* angry. I was *damned* if he was gonna hurt me again. So, I started looking for something to grab, to defend myself with. And then I remembered my insulin in the fridge. I pretended to get the milk out. He was so pissed he never noticed me filling the syringe."

"Maureen? Are *you* hurt?"

She shook her head.

"When I turned to put the milk down I saw him coming for me, and I held on tight to the needle in my cardigan pocket. He flung me to the floor, and the next thing I remember was him pulling me up by my hair, dragging me towards the kettle. Well, there was no way I was gonna let the old bugger burn me again. God help me. He expected me to pull away, but instead, I rose up and stuck him in the neck with the syringe."

Sion inspected Glyn's body. He could see the tiny puncture wound in his neck. A small amount of capillary bleeding had trickled from it but hadn't marked his clothes.

Sion straightened up and went over to her.

"You need to call the police. Tell them what happened. Everything."

A sob escaped, and he held her to him feeling her frail frame as she wept silently against his chest.

"I can't."

"You have to."

Gently pulling himself free, he held her bony shoulder lightly.

"Things are different these days."

She stared up at him.

"Sion, don't pretend I'm not dying. I'm a nurse. I've got three months, six tops. What'll Annie say when she finds out her mam's a murderer?"

She glanced away.

"I want to spend what time I've got left with *her*. I want her home, Sion. Here with me. Will you help me?"

He considered the situation. What choice did he have?

Taking a handkerchief from his pocket, he wet it under the tap. Then, he carefully wiped the blood from Glyn's neck.

"Alright," he found himself answering. "You go to bed and I'll sort it. I'll hang him up in the shed. First thing tomorrow morning, call the police."

"Yes...The police."

He wasn't sure what was registering.

"What are you going to say to them?"

He raised his voice.

"Maureen? This is important."

Glyn stared back at them glassy-eyed like a dead fish on the quarry-tiled floor.

"I'll tell 'em that I thought he'd gone to The Cross Keys. It's what he does most nights. And I'll say how I woke up alone and when he wasn't asleep on the couch, I checked the sheds."

"Good. That'll be fine."

She sniffed.

"And Annie? Can you get Jac to call her, Sion? Tell her to come home."

"We'll sort all that out tomorrow. When the police are here."

Sion's piercing blue eyes met hers.

"This, tonight… it's a very bad thing, there's no denying that. But I promise to do my best for you."

"I know you will, love."

Sion choked back the lump in his throat. It was a mess alright, but he owed it to Maureen. Or was it to his own mother and all the hurt he'd seen as a child and had never been able to stop?

Whatever had made him agree to help, it was past midnight by the time Sion finally got to bed.

And in the lambing shed, hanging from a beam by the same rope that had earlier kept him alive on the rock-face, the corpse of Glyn Evans was dangling in the icy January air.

CHAPTER 1

---------✴---------

Five Months Later

Sion Edwards fixed his eyes on the bare wall behind the detective's head. The video camera in the interview room was on but there was nothing to record. He hadn't said a word. It was how he'd been trained in the special forces. During interrogation, never show even a flicker of a response.

Detective Ellis Roberts began again.

"What I'm interested in is this climbing rope of yours. How did the farmer, your next-door neighbour Glyn Evans get a hold of that rope to kill himself?"

Sion didn't answer.

"Could he have helped himself to your climbing gear? At the cottage perhaps?"

No answer.

"Did you lend him the rope?"

Nothing.

"Come on, Sion. Let's get this over with, yeah? What really happened?"

Silence.

"Look, tell us everything that happened that evening in January. We'll understand. Things happen. Was it an accident?"

The detective sighed.

"For the recording, Sion Edwards refuses to answer the question."

Sion continued to stare straight ahead.

"Okay. Let's try again,"

The detective leaned over the desk towards Sion, his voice rising.

"How did you do it, Sion? How did Glyn Evans die? Did you kill him? Kill him, then hang him up on the beam? Or was he alive when you hanged him?"

A war of silence. No eye contact. One minute, three, five.

"For the recording, Sion Edwards refuses to answer the question."

Fifteen more minutes ticked by. Then Twenty. Now thirty. And still, Sion Edwards stared at the wall, his face fixed in a meditative trance.

The detective slammed his fist onto the desk. "Interview terminated at seven-fifteen pm. Take him back to the cells."

The detective motioned to the uniformed officer at the door then turned back towards Edwards.

"Let's see how a night in the cells improves your communication skills."

Sion stood up without looking at the detective and walked away with the uniformed officer. Hands cuffed behind his back, face impassive.

Draining his coffee Ellis hurled the styrofoam cup at the wall, then rubbed his face. There had to be something more than the rope? All his instinct told him that Sion was involved. But there was nothing in the pathology reports to point to anything other than Glyn Evans committing suicide. The body had been cremated.

Ellis stood up.

And today? How was that connected?

When he'd been called to the hostage situation at The Cross Keys pub earlier that morning. The bar manager had been holding a co-worker, one Claire Williams at knifepoint and he'd slashed her neck badly.

When he got there, the bar manager was already captured, professionally bound up by one Sion Edwards, who'd apparently gone to Claire Williams' rescue.

He'd gone along with the story at first. But then, Ellis had spotted the gun in Edwards' possession. And his heart was in his mouth when he *then* recognised the rope that the bar manager was tied up with. He couldn't believe it.

Sion Edwards, the knight in shining armour, couldn't believe it either when he suddenly found himself arrested for murder.

The detective inspector stood waiting for Roberts as he returned to his workstation. Things weren't going well.

"Got a minute?"

Ellis shrugged and sloped down the corridor after him.

"Shut the door."

The balding inspector sat at his desk, leaning back in his leather chair as Ellis moved a stack of files off the hard plastic seat opposite.

"How long've you been out of uniform? Five years?"

"Thereabouts."

It was seven and this was the first time he'd been called in for 'a chat'.

Stretching his arms behind his head the D.I. revealed two large stained sweat patches as he wound himself up to give the youngster 'the talk.'

"Look, Roberts. Real life's not neat like some detective film. On occasion, we're forced to work in the grey. The long and short of it Ellis is..."

He tapped his pen on the desk.

"We're letting Sion Edwards go."

Ellis cleared his throat. He'd just been told the news. Upstairs had decided it. The case was dropped. Closed.

"'Course, your instincts were bang on. The farmer, using climbing rope to hang himself, it's bloody odd, alright.

"So why're we letting Edwards go, then?"

His boss carried on, oblivious.

"The wife? She died?"

"Yes. Cancer. A few weeks after him."

"Tragic."

The D.I. began the tapping again.

"Well, it's best left to powers higher than us."

He shuffled in his chair, leaning intently across the desk at Ellis.

"You heard of Kingfisher?"

"The National Crime Agency gig? Who hasn't?"

It had been all over the news and internal memos. In a coordinated dawn raid, hundreds of people affiliated to the Scouser gang had received a wake-up call. Police forces across the country had rammed-in front doors, arrested dealers in their beds, tossed houses in the search for drugs and cash.

"Good result," Ellis agreed.

"Better than that. You know that the Scousers use kids as mules. Turning drug deals into takeaway deliveries. Tap the *bleedin'* app. Snow to go."

"Sir? But, what are the Scousers doing here?"

"They're national players these days. And Sion Edwards was a National Crime Agency field operative, our man deep undercover."

The inspector passed a one-page document to Ellis.

"And his intel triggered all those arrests?"

The inspector looked him in the eye.

"Edwards' cover's blown and there's a big price tag on his head. Which is why every scumbag connected to the Scousers, like that dodgy barman today, are trying to take a pop at him. They want him bad."

Ellis frowned as he processed the information.

"So, why isn't he already in witness protection? What's he doin' here?"

"He came to get his girl. This…"

The inspector read the name off his notepad.

"Claire Williams."

"What? Are they together?"

The inspector grinned.

"Not from what the NCA boys were telling me. Sion was trying his luck."

Ellis rubbed the back of his neck.

"And now she's sitting downstairs with stitches down her neck thinking Sion Edwards is a murderer."

"Something like that," the detective inspector agreed grimly. "Like I said, it's a lot messier in real life."

"What d'ya mean you couldn't collect him?"

Connor O'Dwyer, or Irish as he was known on the street, felt the cold chill of his anger icing up inside him as he listened to their excuses. Sion Edwards should be winging his way to him right now. He wasn't interested in their pathetic snivelling about him being arrested.

"We'll pick this up later, when you get back."

He ended the call.

He'd been looking forward all day to finally meeting Sion Edwards. Seeing the little piggy hauled in, strung up and hung upside down on a meat hook in the abattoir that at night was his domain. Watching him wriggling on the hook between the rows of carcasses. Squealing, like the double-crossing runt he was, when he set his eyes on the blade. When he worked out what was about to happen to him.

The stainless steel felt warm in his hand as Irish stroked it and considered his first slice. The straight razor had been his father's weapon of choice. And now it was his. Like father, like son. Slashers both. A reputation carved from flesh.

People would talk about the faces that no longer had ears. The men with permanent smiles cut high into their cheeks. And the snitches silenced, their tongues sliced from their mouths.

His father was long dead. And Connor was known to everyone as 'Irish' now. He'd transformed the Scousers from a raggle-taggle bunch of scallies into the highest-grossing criminal gang in England. He was The General, on the ground running the operation. And to do that, it was vital he kept the fear and the respect alive. Sion Edwards was bad for his reputation.

Yes, he was going to enjoy carving that little piggy up. Sion Edwards, his trusted hitman, a *feckin'* police grass.

He'd post it up online afterwards. Edwards with and without his ears. With and without his snout. And finally, photographed stylishly, his plums resting alongside his tongue on a silver tray.

No one messed with his family and lived. His dad had taught him that. Sion Edwards was the reason his brother Tony was locked away. Not to mention also the millions he'd wiped off the business when the police had raided. His delivery infrastructure was in tatters and his best men banged up. It was going to take months to get fully operational again.

And now, he'd sent his lads all the way to some unpronounceable place where a pub manager said he'd got him. All the idiot had to do was keep Sion Edwards there until they arrived. How hard was that?

Too hard, it turns out. The rat had made total chumps of them. Again.

CHAPTER 2

----------*----------

The rain streams down the outside of the steamed-up taxi window. Wiping a patch clear with my hand, I watch him disappearing from view as we pull out from the police station into the main road.

The pain throbs in my neck like a pulse now the medication has worn off, and I'm dreading removing the dressing. The nurse's face told me enough. The stitches stretch from below my ear to the bottom of my neck. The cut is deep and it's going to scar.

I've been brave all day. But despite my best efforts tears have escaped and are rolling freely down my face matching the rain trickling down the glass.

My empty apartment freaks me out more than it's ever done before and I triple-lock the door and slide the bolt across. Still, I find myself checking each room in turn, flicking the lights on, snapping each set of curtains shut. It's going to take me a while to get over what happened today.

I'm in shock. I'm exhausted too and it's late. But there's no way I'll be sleeping anytime soon.

My flatmate Courtney and her little boy are over at her boyfriend's place again. Nothing's been said but it's only a matter of time before she moves in with him and then I'll be looking for another place. Maybe it's not such a coincidence that my filled backpack is propped up against my wardrobe door.

This morning I'd made up my mind to go with Sion into witness protection. To start a new life together. Now he's gone forever.

After what happened in The Cross Keys today, staying is no longer an option for me either. I need to do it. Go on the world trip I'd been planning and saving hard for before I met Sion.

Met him, I was *barely* with him. We've done a lot of talking. Chatting over the bar. Online. One date. One kiss.

And yet, he's affected me. He's there all the time, swimming through my thoughts.

So confusing.

Serves me right, I suppose. I'd been daring to dream for a while that maybe I'd found someone special. Like Annie finding Jac again after all those years. But I should've known things like that don't happen to girls like me, and Sion was only a fantasy.

And a fantasist? Was he *really* an undercover agent? He was certainly up to his neck in it with a drug gang. My wound still throbs. That was real enough.

The detective called Sion a murderer. But, Annie's father? That's the bit that makes no sense. He couldn't have done it.

The sincerity of his face and my betrayal.

Even with my eyes closed, I can still see the way he looked at me. Hear the crack in his voice as he pleaded with me to go with him.

"We've got something, you and me. Something I've never felt before with anyone else. Tell me you don't feel it too? Come with me, Claire. Why won't you come? I'm innocent."

And I hear my voice answering him. Its hardness slices through him worse than the blade on my neck.

"Because… I'm not sure I believe you."

I can't unsay it, and it cleaves us instantly apart.

It haunts me. Him standing by the police station entrance, watching as I climb into the taxi. As I drive away.

I pour hot water onto a camomile teabag. Taking the steaming cup through, I sit down on my bed, the last few hours replaying like a boomerang video in my head.

My body shudders as I feel myself held hostage again, gripped tightly by the hair. Head pulled back, the coldness of the metal against my exposed neck. Then, the vicious slash. Slicing into my skin as I struggled to break free. And Sion leaping on him from out of nowhere. Pulling me free. Overpowering the barman and tying him up... Saving me.

"Oww!"

Hot tea splashes onto my thigh.

My hands are shaking uncontrollably.

Gripping the mug I place it onto the bedside table and try deep breathing.

I've made a massive mistake.

Maybe, it's not too late? Surely there's still time to catch up with him, meet him in London before he goes? Say I'm sorry. Tell him I love him?

Reaching for my phone, I try a text.

'I believe you. I'm sorry. Can I still come? Claire x'

The message bounces back. Three times. His phone clicks off when I call and there's no voicemail. His social media accounts have vanished.

It's too late. Sion Edwards is officially no more.

My silent tears turn into a full-on meltdown. Even though I'm still fully dressed, I wrap myself in my quilt, cocooning my sore neck in the soft pillow. A shiver runs through me. I was lucky to walk away with a cut, they said. But the truth is my heart's completely broken. And it's all my doing.

The bunch of keys clattered onto the airport cafeteria table.

"So... Mr Cobain..."

He couldn't help but catch the slight smirk that flashed across the British Consulate official's face as he said it.

"Alright, don't laugh, it was the first name I thought of. Look, I was under pressure to come up with something quickly."

He'd persuaded them to keep his first name Sion with a new spelling, but then the choice of surname had completely stumped him. Until he remembered Claire's favourite band, that was. And after that he was re-christened. Sion Edwards was dead. He was now Shaun Cobain.

Stifling a yawn, he picked up the house keys.

"So, where's this place again?"

"Three hours up to Dargarei from Auckland and then another hour or so northwest through the forest and you're there."

Shaun clicked and rolled his neck. A four-hour drive was the last thing he needed right now after his mammoth flight. It was a good job he'd slept on the plane but he'd be kidding himself if he said that he wasn't jet-lagged.

"There's a car parked for you in the short stay. Don't expect too much. Government funding isn't what it was."

The civil servant produced a plastic bag from his briefcase and slid it across the table towards Shaun.

He examined inside then pulled out a set of car keys, a mobile phone and a charger.

"The address of the place is in your contacts under 'Home'."

Shaun grinned.

"Of course."

The civil servant smiled back.

"We aim to please. And if you need anything urgently, then call the number under 'Mummy'."

"Sweet."

"*Aha!* You've picked up the Kiwi lingo already."

Shaun took out a brown envelope from inside the bag. He'd already been given a passport with New Zealand residency before he left London.

As he carefully tore the top open he could see that they'd given him a new UK driving licence too, plus a bunch of papers including his new birth certificate.

Shaun raised an eyebrow as he shuffled through them.

"A degree? In sport and fitness?"

"Granted, it's a bit of a stretch, we figured you might need it to get work."

"But I joined the army at sixteen?"

He'd promised himself that there'd be no more lies.

"Then, you've probably done a degree's worth of training and fitness."

That was true. But still, it didn't sit right with him. He wanted to live his new life honestly.

Shaun produced another set of papers. This time, it was a land registry map stapled to the top of another document.

"The deeds to a house?"

Shaun flicked through the pages.

"And there's land with it too?"

The consulate official shrugged.

"Call it a severance payment from Her Majesty. We don't use it anymore."

He added hastily, "Anyway, it's been decided. It's all yours, and I don't mind telling you that you've landed yourself quite a bargain."

Shaun studied the documentation. He'd never dropped lucky in his life before. An embassy residence. That sounded pretty fancy.

He pictured a large, white-washed colonial mansion with a wrap-around porch and a sweet-smelling climbing rose around the door. He imagined himself sitting on a swing seat with a bottle of cold beer watching the sunset between snow-capped New Zealand mountain peaks.

And there was land too. The map outlined a large parcel of ground stretching back behind the property. It didn't show any detail but something like that must surely be worth a few pennies.

The civil servant was right though, it *was* the least they could do, under the circumstances. After all, he'd helped them clear the most notorious of all the Albanian gangs out of London. And thanks to him, a good chunk of the Scouser network that had moved onto the patch afterwards had been convicted. He'd passed on vital information about their logistics and how the Scousers used encrypted phones and sites on the dark web so that all their future communications could be hacked too. It was dynamite intel on England's most sophisticated gang.

All in all quite a coup for the National Crime Agency. And he'd risked everything to give it to them. The Scousers were an unforgiving bunch of psychos. Sitting here on the other side of the world, Sion was paying the price. And Claire was too.

Claire. He felt an unfamiliar pang deep within him when he thought about her. He was gutted that she'd gone. Forever, she'd be thinking that he'd murdered Glyn Evans. Her friend Annie's father. That hurt worse than any jab in the gut.

He'd gladly hand it all back to see Claire again. She'd made it clear that she didn't want anything more to do with him. But, for some reason, even though they could never meet or speak again, convincing Claire that he was innocent mattered to him more than anything else.

"To get to the property, you'll need to head north out of Auckland. Then pick up a few supplies in Dargarei on the way through. It's your last town before you hit the forest. There's been no one living in the property for a while so you'll have to make do for a night or two until you get settled."

"No problem for an old soldier like me," Shaun joked. "I'm used to bushcraft and surviving in the wilderness."

The civil servant coughed nervously.

"Good."

"And what about work?"

The civil servant drained his coffee and shifted in his seat, making ready to leave.

"We've fixed you up with something part-time in a school further north, up the coast. It'll get you started. Give them a call once you've settled in. The details are on the phone."

"But, I'm not a teacher."

"It'll be helping out, that kind of thing. Don't worry."

Great. The only thing he knew about kids was that he was one himself once. And a pretty messed up one, at that. He'd never much attended any of the three different high schools he'd been signed up for. His social worker had called him 'schoolphobic'. At the time, he thought they'd made the term up.

Still, a job was a job and it would do until he found something else. Building work, plumbing or joinery perhaps? He'd done lots of that before.

Shaun rolled the keys in his hand. With a consulate residency in the middle of paradise, who cared? He'd do anything as long as he could have some time outdoors biking, kayaking, climbing.

The security services had told him from the off that they didn't want to know about his undercover earnings, and his offshore account had more money in it than he could ever imagine spending. So he wasn't going to sweat about the school thing.

As he slid the documents back into the envelope he noticed a glossy photographic paper stuck to the inside.

"Who's this?"

He put the photograph between them on the table. It showed a freckled, dark-haired man with a snub nose. Mid-thirties, he'd guess. The photo had been snapped of him in front of a pub. He had a cigarette in his fingertips and he was talking into a mobile phone.

"Ah! You've found him. That's Connor O'Dwyer. Known on the street as Irish."

Shaun bristled.

"Irish?"

It was the name of his Scouser contact. The contact that had tried to trap him before.

Seeing his face for the first time was strange. Irish looked quite ordinary. Hardly the ruthless sociopath he'd heard him to be. And it was obvious he'd never been arrested if this was the best photograph they had of him. That meant he was super-smart too.

"Why the picture?"

Shaun watched the pen-pusher squirming. There was something he was holding out on.

"It's a precaution, that's all. So you'll recognise him."

"Why do I need to?"

The civil servant sighed.

"He's extended the contract on you. He's made it international."

Shaun weighed it up. He was far enough away not to be worried about that. He drained his coffee in one gulp.

"I promise, if I hear a scouse accent within a hundred feet of me, I'll run."

"We think it's unlikely that he'll leave the UK. But be warned, there are several criminal gangs over here and in Australia too who'd be very interested if they got wind of you popping up on their patch."

Getting up to leave, the civil servant put his arms through his jacket sleeves, then reached for his soft leather briefcase.

"It should be safe enough out here. But, have your wits about you, Cobain. With global connectivity, witness protection isn't what it was. O'Dwyer's brother's facing a ten-year stretch because of you. He's a bitter man. You've hurt his family and he wants you dead."

CHAPTER 3

---------*---------

"So, you've got me dressed like a total nob-head. Made me spend a fortune on these sticks. What's so important that you've had to drag me out here?"

Irish's long-time friend and business partner Peter set the golf ball onto the tee.

"They're clubs."

"What?"

Peter selected the driver from the bag.

"The sticks? They're called clubs."

Settling his feet square to the ball Peter practised his swing moving his hips fluidly as the driver arched into the air.

He squared himself up and then did it again. This time for real. It was how Peter Caruthers played everything in life. Precise with no margin for error.

Irish's eyes followed the ball as it was sent in a perfect trajectory towards the flag on the far green.

"Not bad."

The two of them had started their operation up as students. He had met Peter on his first day at university.

He'd booked a room in the halls of residence even though he lived a few miles up the road. The idea had been to get a bit of space from who he really was. Make a fresh start at university. Turned out, he'd been put into an accommodation block with a complete bunch of wankers who'd all been on gap years, jollying it up in Thailand and Bali. Hooray Henrys from posh private schools.

He'd nearly jacked it all in there and then. Business and Economics. His school had pushed him into it. What was he doing? The boy from Bootle who lived in a terraced house near the docks. The boy whose dad was spoken about in hushed tones.

And there, next door to his room, sitting on his immaculately-made up bed was Peter. Quiet and well-spoken, he'd smiled at Connor and asked him if he wanted to go with him to the Student Union that evening for a pint.

And that was that. By the end of the month Connor was sourcing and selling weed and blow to all the Hoorays, and posh-boy Peter was investing their cash into a diverse portfolio of start-ups and stocks. They were cleaning up. Big time.

It was in their second year that they cooked up their business model. County lines they'd called it. It was essentially a supply chain that got their drugs right across the country using dealer hubs, drug mules and text messaging. Simple, but no one had ever taken the street deal into carefully planned logistics before. And with their combined skill sets and Connor's connections, they knew they could swing it.

And now fifteen years on, Peter lived in a gated mansion in Cheshire. His kids went to private school and did pony club on the weekends. No one would ever think that Peter Caruthers was the Scousers' Chief Operating Officer, handling millions of pounds of drug imports and money laundering.

Connor lined the ball onto the tee. He took the Big Bertha out of his bag and practised the shot, carefully copying his friend.

This time it was for real. Swinging back, he gave it an almighty thump.

The ball sliced out of bounds over into the trees lining the edge of the fairway.

Pete gave Connor a patient smile. He knew how much Irish hated golf.

"Why bring me all the way out here?"

"I needed space around us. Clothes that aren't bugged."

He gave his friend a sarcastic stare. Peter had picked them out for him. Left for him at the reception desk. A pink golfing polo shirt, lemon diamond-knit sweater and light grey trousers. He'd done it on purpose. Chosen the colours to wind him up. Only Pete was allowed to do that.

Everything Irish had with him, phones included, had been left in the locker room.

He stared at his friend.

"Why? What's up?"

"I think our operation's been compromised. The second Dutch container was raided yesterday. Could be a coincidence, but, put it this way... one raid's unusual. But two in a row?"

"How much?"

"Ten million."

"*Jees.*"

Irish felt a little queasy as they started walking up the fairway towards the first ball. His. It was only money. But still.

"Look, are you sayin' we got another leak? Or are we being bugged?"

"That's the thing, Irish. I put a different team on the second consignment."

"So?"

"I think the NCA's monitoring our phones."

"What, the Encrochat? Thought you said it was safe?"

"I did... but I don't wanna take any risks. We need to go back to old school."

That meant meetups like this one. More *feckin'* golf. It meant regularly swapped burner phones and using different dark web chat rooms. It was a blag and it would slow them down. How could the National Crime Agency have found their devices?

Irish sniffed.

"Sion Edwards."

"'Scuse me?"

"*Sion Edwards...* He had one of the Encrochat phones. He's an NCA operative. They've used it to hack us."

The hitman was screwing with the whole operation.

Wherever he was, Irish vowed he'd never rest until Sion Edwards was his. Hanging from a hook.

The traffic was easing as Shaun headed over the spectacular Auckland flyovers. Hugging the coast, wending his way north in the black BMW estate that he'd been given.

It was winter here, but New Zealand was still warm; the vegetation, a lush chlorophyllic green.

He'd chosen this country because Claire had told him that she'd wanted to visit it someday. Her father was a Kiwi. Not that she'd ever met him.

He'd no idea what the place would be like. He'd been clutching at straws trying to cling onto the futile hope that he might meet up with her again, even though he knew he never could. But, simply being here he felt a little more connected to her.

And he'd made a good choice. New Zealand was stunningly beautiful.

He drove off the highway into a pretty little town and onwards down to the beach road to drink a can of coke and eat the takeaway pie that he'd bought in the garage a few miles back.

He hadn't been sure about the beef in gravy with cheese combo, but the pie tasted surprisingly good after a day and night of airline food.

Scrunching up the paper and foil, he got out of the car and headed for the litter bin he'd spotted, then continued down to the white sand cove below the road.

A few hundred metres in front of the empty beach, bursting out from the calm aquamarine ocean was a small clump of land, a tiny uninhabited island crammed full of thick bushes and trees.

For some reason, seeing the lush little piece of land sprouting from the sea made him feel even more alone.

Not that many people would miss him. His mother overdosed when he was twenty-one and his dad had left when he was a kid. Told them he was going away to work on the oil rigs out in Saudi. He'd heard years later that his dad had been shacked up twenty miles away with another woman the whole time and that they'd had a kid together. Good luck to them, he thought bitterly. He hoped he'd been a better dad the second time around.

The only family he'd ever known had been the army, and his brothers in arms, Jac and Jason. Jac had moved out of the cottage where they'd both been staying. He was a proper Welsh sheep farmer now, living in the farmhouse with Maureen's daughter, Annie. And Jason had swapped flying helicopters in and out of Helmand for huge passenger airliners in and out of Singapore. And now, Shaun had lost his special forces brothers too.

The landscape was becoming more and more rural the further north he drove. And the traffic was thinning out with only the odd lorry and car sharing the road.

He passed through steep valleys covered in huge tree ferns and straight-trunked trees that seemed to stretch infinitely into the sky.

He wouldn't be surprised to see a pterodactyl flying above him or a dinosaur popping out from the dense, prehistoric bush surrounding him.

And then the landscape changed again. And now he was driving through rolling, volcanic, dairy pastures littered with hundreds of ginger cows.

Shaun rubbed his neck to ease the stiffness and pain that was starting to set in as he carried on driving west past a small town declaring itself to be the sweet potato capital of the world.

And then on to Dargarei, a sprawling agricultural town on the banks of a mighty muddy river. Passing tractor dealerships and farmers' merchants on the outskirts, he pushed on to the centre and parked up on the main street.

Boxy shops scruffily lined this long, one-street, one-horse town. Colonial clapperboard frontages popped out from behind modern signage as if a Hollywood western had been shot here and they'd hastily covered over the set. And at the bottom of the main drag, a Victorian heap of a hotel claimed itself to be the town's sports bar. The place felt like an outpost that was never quite tamed and was now overlooked in favour of the prettier east coast.

Shaun was still thinking about how he'd landed in the Wild West as he picked up a sleeping bag and took it over to the counter in the camping and fishing shop.

The check-shirted man behind the desk raised an eyebrow as he scanned the label on the sleeping bag.

"That it?"

Shaun signalled an acknowledgement. The beds wouldn't be aired, but he didn't think he'd be slumming it.

"Not fishing, then?"

"No."

"Good as gold."

The man appraised Shaun carefully.

"Goin' camping?"

"Something like that."

"Weekend away in the bush, eh?"

"Hmm."

"Where you planning on heading?"

Shaun scratched the back of his head and sighed to himself resignedly. This dude wasn't giving up.

"Look, do you know this place?"

He held out his phone for the shopkeeper to read the address.

"Lake Lodge?"

He took in the store owner's blank face and switched the map app on for him.

"Ahh, okay... I see... it looks like Jake's Place."

"Jake? Does someone live there?"

"No. Not now. No one's lived there since... well... since he passed."

Before Shaun could ask more, the man cut the conversation dead, then disappeared underneath the counter to rummage through boxes of stock.

His dishevelled head re-emerged a few seconds later and he clanked a large hunting knife onto the sales desk in front of them.

Shaun stared hard at the long sheathed knife, then looked intently at the man.

"What's that for?"

The store owner shrugged but met him square in the eye.

"Might come in handy up there."

Shaun had heard of upselling. A cake with a coffee, chocolates at the till, but this was the oddest thing he'd ever been offered.

"Nah, you're fine."

"You sure?"

Shaun nodded.

The knife disappeared back into the box below the counter.

"Your call, mate."

"So…" Shaun tried again, "This Lake Lodge, or uh, Jake's Place? What's it like?"

"Middle of the wop wops. By the lake."

The store owner ended the conversation brusquely and Shaun handed over his new bank card.

The man smiled a little more kindly at him as he processed the payment.

"Look, you seem like a nice fulla. If it's a pretty camping spot to stay for the weekend you're after, you're best headin' over to The Bay of Islands. Keri Keri, Russell; it's beautiful out that way. And they're much more geared up for tourists like yourself. Where you're heading, it's a bit… a bit wild. Not so many people, no police. Got all sorts livin' up there."

Shaun tapped his pin into the card reader.

"No. I'm going to the Lodge."

It was a well-meant warning but he was more than capable of handling himself against a couple of wild men in the woods.

The shop owner shrugged and handed him back his card folded neatly in the paper receipt.

"Suit yourself."

With groceries and his new sleeping bag, Shaun got back on the road, following the route planner on his phone.

He eased his car tentatively through a never-ending string of jersey cows crossing the road on their way to being milked. The man in the store was right, where he was heading was rural.

Gradually, as he headed further northwest, the farms petered out and the ancient fern trees and native bush began to close in again.

The roads were becoming rougher too and it took all of Shaun's concentration to avoid the potholes and small heaps of shale that were more frequently littering the highway.

Heavily laden forestry lorries passed by. But it didn't look like many people lived out here. Still, it was perfect for an embassy retreat. And a perfect hideout for him, a place to start over.

Maybe even farm?

Thinking about how Jac would laugh at that made him feel sad.

Finally, the map app told him to turn.

Shaun pulled up and checked the route. It was pointing him off the road, up a dusty track into the forest. It was rough gravel, but looking at the online map he didn't have much choice.

The underneath of the car scraped disconcertingly against stones as he scrunched over the unsealed road, trying to avoid the deep ruts washed out by rain.

The BMW clanked again as he hit another hole. He prayed that it wasn't the radiator. The BMW was holding out, but he'd be wise to trade it for an off-roader.

The track was taking him deeper into the forest and away from any sign of civilisation. He was certain there were no wild hoodlums around here, not with a road this bad.

Suddenly, after a twist in the road, he spotted a clearing and fields. And then, as he turned the next bend he saw it. A large, pristine turquoise lake lined with long stretches of white sand.

The pin for his destination was right on the lake shoreline. He scanned the edge of the lake for the embassy residence, but he couldn't see any buildings.

Slowly, the road neared the lake and he followed the track around the shore, passing a sandy beach. There were two picnic benches there, though the place was deserted today.

His eyes combed the bush for the property.

You have now reached your destination.

Shaun turned another bend. And then he saw it. There, on the shoreline ahead of him, stood an impressively forbidding, almost gothic-looking dark timbered lodge.

It certainly didn't look like a home. The windows on one side and the back door were boarded up with chipboard which someone had sprayed with graffiti drawings and tags.

Closer inspection didn't make it look any more welcoming. The dark, rambling house was surrounded at the rear and the side by clumps of giant grasses and bushes that gave way to paddocks, once cleared, but now reclaimed by the scrub and weeds.

A large wooden barn to the side looked intact, but would it hold stock? And he didn't even want to think about the state of the fences.

Stepping back, he examined the lodge. An additional wing on each side of the main building jutted out like a mad architect's afterthought. Vegetation sprouted out from the ancient guttering, and even from here he could see a large hole in the rusty zinc-sheeted roof on the left-hand side.

He made his way onto the old porch that wrapped around the front, avoiding two perilous holes where the planks had rotted and given way.

There was no rambling rose. Or swing-seat to drink a cold beer and gaze out at the lake. The place needed a hell of a lot of work.

He couldn't see in, the windows at the front were shuttered up from the inside. Across the boarded-up kitchen window, a magnificently paint-sprayed cobra reared up in attack, its forked tongue smelling him out as Shaun began pulling the chipboard free from its tacks.

The board came away in his hands revealing the glass-lined edges of a smashed-in window, big enough for someone to get in and out.

Peering inside, he could see that squatters had indeed been in there.

On the floor, there was a sizable collection of empty bottles and beer cans. This place may be deserted now, but it had evidently been vandalised and used as a camp at some point.

The store owner was right, this was a place beyond the law.

With some reluctance, he tried the keys in the lock, willing each one not to fit. But depressingly one did.

His heart sank. This was it.

This was what he'd been given for all his sacrifices for Queen and Country. A twenty-seven hour flight and a four-hour drive to the ends of the earth, to find himself the proud owner of a derelict squatters' den.

CHAPTER 4

---------*---------

"You again?"

"Uh, yeah."

Shaun squirmed slightly as he felt the shop owner's eyes on him. He'd driven the hour back to town to try and catch the shops before they shut, and now the camping store guy was making him feel like a naughty child.

He'd been right, though. It would have been better if he'd have gone east to one of the tourist towns.

"Seen Jake's Place for yourself, did ya?"

Shaun nodded.

"Hmm. I'm gonna need a few more things."

"Mess was it?"

"Yeah, you could say that. It wasn't exactly what I was expecting. It's gonna take a few days to sort. Who exactly was this Jake?"

Was it something he said? Shaun looked on surprised as the man promptly turned his back to him and disappeared into the private area behind the desk, leaving Shaun alone at the counter.

Bloody rude.

Shaun shook his head and drifted over towards the camping stoves. He'd be needing something to cook on until he got the electricity connected. And pots and a kettle. A cup and a plate. He spotted a camping chair on special offer too that would come in handy.

"Right. That's all sorted," the shopkeeper announced, strolling up to him.

"Excuse me?"

"I've squared it with the Team Leader."

"Team Leader?"

"Celia. The Missus. You're staying at ours."

He stretched his hand out towards him before Shaun had a chance to respond.

"I'm Frank. Frank Plunkett, good to meet ya'."

"Err...Sion. Sion Ed..." He coughed. "Sorry, I'm Shaun Cobain, pleased to meet you too."

"Not often we get Poms straying up to these parts."

"I'm Welsh."

Much to Shaun's surprise, Frank slapped him on the back.

"Well, why the bloody hell didn't ya say? We gave you guys a fair ole whippin' last season."

Shaun smirked. The universal language of sport. Wales had toured New Zealand last year and had gotten a thrashing.

"Best not mention the rugby. You guys were awesome."

Frank's face broke into a broad grin.

"Well, that's settled it. A rugby fan. You're coming back to ours, no argument. Celia's making up the bed in the sleepout for ya and I'm sure I got some of them Lions games recorded."

"Oh, I couldn't possibly..."

"Nonsense. 'Course ya can. It's a damn sight better than staying up on yer own in the middle of bloody nowhere. We're on the road to the lake about a half-hour north of here."

The jet lag was starting to kick in and Shaun wasn't going to fight it.

"Frank, it's incredibly kind of you. Thank you."

"No worries, mate. It's how we are 'round here. Celia's making a pot roast, so I 'spect you'll be wantin' a feed too."

"That'd be great."

"We'll get ya sorted. Right now, seems to me you could do with a shower and an early night?"

Shaun wasn't going to argue.

"I'm about done here."

He winked at Shaun.

"Had more than my fair share of Pommy campers for one day."

Irish shifted his feet as he queued in the line of visitors to see his brother. For a new prison, the security procedures were pretty rudimentary, lax even, with only a cursory sweep of a handheld metal detector over his body and the nebulous threat of a latex finger up his arse if they suspected him of concealing drugs.

But he was still taking a huge risk.

"You can't take that in."

The security guard at the front of the queue nodded towards the magazine in Irish's hand.

"Ah, come on, Sir. It's only a magazine," he pleaded persuasively in a thick Liverpudlian accent he hammed up especially for the occasion. "Thought reading was good for ya la', when you're banged up behind bars."

The guard signalled to the sign behind him.

No drugs. No alcohol. No cigarettes. No food. No drink. No phones.

"It's only a bike mag. *Ahhh*, go on, Sir, don't be tight. Have a skeck yourself, if ya want?"

He held out the motorcycle magazine for the prison officer who gave it a good shake and flicked through the pages, examining them carefully.

"It's his birthday next week, he's mad on motorbikes, our kid."

"It'll be a good few birthdays before he gets one of these," the officer sneered.

Irish played along in friendly agreement.

"Yeah, bet we'll all be ridin' bleedin' hoverboards by the time he gets out, the poor sod."

The prison officer's face cracked a fraction as he handed it back to him.

He eyeballed Irish.

"Go on with yer, this once. But no more magazines, alright?"

Irish nodded back at him gratefully. He was fully aware of the business card that had been slipped inside the pages and he made sure that the guard saw that he'd tipped it into his hand before stowing it discreetly away in his pocket.

On the card he was sure that there'd be details of where to put the payment later, probably a PayPal account.

He grinned gratefully at the guard.

"Thanks, Officer. It'll make his day."

The bastards. It was the same everywhere. It felt like the whole lot of them were on the take.

Wandering over with the group of families and children to the large visitor hall he spotted his younger brother sitting on a plastic chair at one of the middle rows of tables.

Tony was like the rest of them now. Gone was his sharp look and the designer brands. His hair badly needed a cut and he was dressed in a prison regulation stone-grey sweatshirt paired with saggy jersey joggers.

"Our Tony! How you doin' lad?"

Irish hugged his brother briefly, aware that a prison officer was hovering hawkishly nearby.

"Brought you a little pressie."

He handed him the magazine.

Tony took it and raised an eyebrow.

"Ta."

Irish winked.

"No dirty pics in this one. Only bikes."

They both knew that every page was soaked with highly addictive synthetic marijuana. The prison's psychoactive drug of choice.

The heavily tattooed lifer sat at the table next to them knew it too, and stole a shifty glance their way.

"Make sure you keep it safe, yeah?"

Irish spoke a little more loudly for the benefit of their earwigging friend to the left.

"This place is full of robbin' bastards."

Tony smirked as his neighbour's eyes promptly shifted away. He flicked through the magazine doing the calculations in his head. Each page cut up and sold in small squares was worth hundreds.

"Can you get me next month's edition too?"

"Ya don't ask much do ya? I'll see what I can do."

Irish lowered his voice to a murmur.

"Did ya get on the cleaning gig like I said?"

"Yeah."

"Good lad."

Being a cleaner was a ticket to ride. It meant you could go everywhere, across the floors into different wings, even into cells. It was the perfect job for a man who needed to make discreet deliveries.

"You managed to find him yet, Irish?"

His eyes narrowed. Thirty families without lads and dads, all doing long stretches in prison. The man who'd put his little brother inside, Sion Edwards was a professional ghost. He'd been elusive enough when he'd been their hired gun. But after the botched grab in the pub by that idiot barman, he'd disappeared completely off the grid.

He'd put the word out and he'd gone big on the reward. He wasn't messing about here. He sent a clear message that he wanted the rat found, and there were ten big ones for a location and another hundred for anyone who could keep him there to be collected and killed.

Throughout the UK, even onto the continent, if Sion Edwards put so much as a single toe down anywhere between Liverpool and Larnaca, he'd have him.

With so much dosh being offered, there'd been a few unreliable sightings from across his British network, but all of them had been quickly dismissed and the trail had gone stone cold.

The reality was that the grass was probably already in witness protection in some far-flung place. Whether he was in Nova Scotia or Nowheresville Nebraska, Sion Edwards had become Irish's obsession. He was unfinished business and he intended to personally find him in the name of his brother.

The only other link to Sion Edwards was Claire Williams, the bird who'd got her neck sliced. She'd blindly added his fake profile to her social media accounts and he was watching them closely. Not bad on the eye either from the pictures he'd seen. Long, dark hair and olive coloured skin. Nice tits.

There hadn't been anything of interest from her as of yet. She was back working behind the bar at that pub.

But he could guarantee one thing, everyone made a mistake eventually. And when she did, he'd be ready.

"Crystal's husband's Greek and he's got me a job at his brother's café in Crete. They need English speaking waiting-on staff."

"Seems like you've got summer sorted."

"Yeah, I've handed in my notice here."

Annie takes a sip of her beer as I tell her my news. A Facebook friend has come through for me. It's a quiet night in The Cross Keys.

I lean across the bar to her.

"To be honest, this place's creeping me out."

I glance over at the new bar manager. She's been good to me since the attack but I'm still nervous about the place. Especially at nights on my turn to lock up.

It's only The Cross Keys, I keep telling myself. A country pub. But even so, I can't help but get the feeling that I'm being watched.

Strangers keep coming in. Men on their own. Drinking one pint slowly, studying their phones or reading a paper. I'm sure I've never noticed that happening before. Or is it me, projecting my fears?

One guy was reading a copy of the Liverpool Echo. I completely lost it, when I saw that. I couldn't stop shaking. It is probably in my head, which also confirms that it's time for a change of scenery.

Annie covers my hand with hers on the bar top. Her face is full of concern.

"Claire, I think you've got some post-traumatic stress."

"No. It's nothing. I'll get over it."

"Jac says it's more common than people realise. He had it after his truck got blown to bits in Afghanistan. He had counselling. You need to get some too. It'll help."

Jac's playing a game of pool with two lads from school. He looks perfectly sane to me. He looks much happier these days. It gives me hope that I can get over this too.

"I'll be better when I'm away from here. I'm ready for a new start, Annie."

She smiles at me. She's been there too.

CHAPTER 5

--------*--------

Shaun had stayed two days at Frank and Celia's place.

The first night, he'd tasted Celia's delicious roast beef dinner, drank a glass of crisp Marlborough sauvignon and promptly crashed.

He'd been out for the count. And in his deep sleep he'd found himself back in the fox hole in the Helmand dust. Machine-guns rattling around his head, stuck, unable to move. Hunkering down as small as he could. Scared shitless that at any moment a bullet would catch him.

He jumped awake with a start.

His eyes took a second to focus, his heart to stop pumping. His muscles were taut, ready to punch.

Where the hell was he? It was late. Mid-morning.

The sound he'd heard was a heavy clattering coming from something on top of the zinc roof.

Then he remembered. He was in Frank and Celia's converted shed at the bottom of their garden. A sleepout, they called it.

When he emerged outside he saw the culprits. The garden was teeming with birds. Strange ones that he came later to know as myna birds and fantails. And more familiar ones, like a king-fisher who sat as bold as brass on the branch of a heavily-laden grapefruit tree.

After lunch, Frank got his assistant to close up and insisted on taking Shaun out fishing.

"You're not a proper Kiwi 'til you've got a rod in your hand," he told Shaun. "And today we're gonna chuck a line off the beach. The offshore wind's sweet as."

He took a box of bait out of the fridge in the shed.

"Make yerself useful will ya and grab us that chilly bin."

He howled with laughter as he registered Shaun's total confusion.

"Chilly bin … Mate? *The beers!*"

Shaun rolled his eyes and took the coolbox of beers out to the pickup truck. Screwed to the flatbed was a large winch.

"Bloody hell, Frank. How big are these fish?"

Frank grinned.

"You'll see."

He drove Shaun out towards the beach over a rough gravel track, then down through what Shaun would class as more of a dry riverbed than a road.

Holding the wheel tightly and managing the gears, Frank skilfully guided the truck as it slipped and skidded down the steep sandy gully onto the vast sandy beach below.

Miles and miles of rugged, deserted west coast beach stretched each way into a gloriously sunny haze. And in front of him, Shaun counted ten lines of waves pounding the shore relentlessly in fierce walls of surf.

The sand was compacted and Frank drove easily along it waving at the odd fisherman as they went.

On they drove, past a craggy outcrop and along more beach, pausing occasionally to study the waves until they found what Frank assessed to be the perfect fishing spot.

"We'll stick the ute here."

Frank swung the pickup around so that the flatbed faced the waves.

"D'ya like yer nose?"

Shaun looked back at him.

"Yeah. I guess?"

"Well, if you do, you'd better get used to wearing these."

He threw him a soft-brimmed Tilley hat and a bottle of sun

lotion.

"Hole in the *bloody* ozone right above us. Too many of my mates have had melanomas. That fair Pommy skin of yours'll get burned to a crisp in no time."

Doing as he was told, Shaun put the hat on and applied the suncream onto his face while Frank got the lines together.

Then, Frank patiently instructed him on how to prepare the kite and bait lines onto the winch, casting far out across the boiling surf. The kite took the lines out further into the ocean beyond the shore, aided by the offshore winds.

When Shaun tried it he caught nothing, but Frank snagged three decent-sized red snappers that any fisherman would have been proud of, except for Frank. It was a pretty average catch he grumbled, passing Shaun a cold beer. But it would do for their supper.

The next afternoon Shaun stood with Frank and Celia, keys in hand on the steps of the rotten porch at the lake lodge.

Celia, a small red-haired Irish-looking lady with boundless energy, had a pen and a large pad of paper at the ready. She'd already begun making a list of things that Shaun could do with. It had pretty much everything on there already, and they hadn't even gone in yet.

"And you're not getting a shipment, ya say?" she probed.

"No."

"Most of you Poms when ya come out here, you ship your stuff out too."

"This place was given to me."

It was tricky. Shaun was answering as truthfully as he could.

"And no family back home?"

"No. I was in the army."

He was beginning to feel a little hot under the collar. He needed to close down Celia's digging.

"Hey, Frank. Can you fish this lake?"

"You're dead right you can, in season."

Frank had taken the bait.

"Best trout you'll find, this side of Auckland. You can try a fly off the shoreline but the fish here go deep, it's best in a boat."

Celia huffed.

"Obsessed!"

"You never complain when I bring fish home."

"I do when you're too bone idle to gut 'em."

Turning the key in the kitchen door, they all made their way in tramping over Shaun's footprints in the dust and carefully stepping over the piles of empty bottles.

Celia sniffed.

"Kids, I'll bet. They come up here in summer to camp out and drink. I'm pretty sure it's not squatters. 'Sides, who'd wanna stay here after dark, unless you wanted to be scared?"

Her words trailed off as Frank threw her a look.

Shaun hadn't appeared to hear that. He'd opened a kitchen cupboard and was surprised to see that it was neatly stacked with piles of matching crockery. The place was fully kitted out.

"Hey, you can scratch half of your list, Celia. Look, there's pans, plates, cutlery. Everything's here."

Celia followed him, working her way through the cupboards.

"Well, who'd a thought it?"

Shaun turned to Celia.

"Did ya know Jake?"

Celia coughed.

"Err... I think he was... err... the caretaker for the place... *eh, Frank*?"

"Yeah, that's right. Years ago."

Shaun opened more drawers. Cloths in one, batteries and string in another and one with cooking equipment in. All tidily stored away and clean.

"And no one's lived here since?"

"Not that I know of."

"Well, everything's been left intact," Shaun surmised, checking and finding that the ancient fridge and freezer were all empty and cleaned out.

Someone had cleaned up after Caretaker Jack had passed. No tins or packets of food had been left, nothing that could rot.

And now that he'd slept, the place didn't look quite so bad. They were in a spacious kitchen area. It was dated and needed a damn good clean but it had all the basics, and there was a large range for cooking and heating the water.

It looked like after Jack the Caretaker had died, the British Consulate had simply sent in the cleaners, then locked the door and forgotten about the place.

He turned the tap. Nothing for a second, then suddenly with a heavy knocking of pipes came a spluttering, followed by a steady flow of water into the sink. It wasn't hot, but at least he had running water.

"What happened to Jake?"

Celia was picking up the bottles, and Frank had his head stuck behind the fridge, busy trying to find the plug and socket.

"Died."

Shaun tried the door through to the next room. It was locked.

"At least the kids couldn't get any further into the house."

Shaun tried each of his keys in turn until he eventually found one that opened it.

Wandering through into the darkness of the next room, Celia grabbed Frank's hand apprehensively.

The kids called Jake's Place 'the haunted house.' But no ghosts were required. The story of the police grim findings was enough to make the hairs stand up on the back of her neck. Imagining what happened here creeped her out.

Celia whispered under her breath to Frank.

"Was it here they....?"

He squeezed her hand in affirmation but kept tight-lipped as they found themselves in the main lounge behind Shaun.

He swiped the torch on his new phone and scanned the room.

"Hold on."

Frank saw Shaun going over to the shuttered windows and promptly gave him a hand to open them up.

The effect was instant.

The light streaming in bounced onto the rimu wood that lined the floors and ceiling, flooding the room with warm, golden light.

Shaun was speechless. The place was stunning.

"*Ah!* It's clean."

Frank frowned at Celia.

"I mean, *wow!*"

She rushed over to the full-length windows and stood beside her husband.

"The view. It's a beaut."

Frank looked out towards the lake.

"I'll say. Who'd have thought it, eh? And I've lived out this way since I was a nipper. Needs a fair amount of fixin' up, but she'll be right."

"Yes, she will," Shaun agreed, taking in the large living room with its high vaulted ceilings and large, stone chimney breast. In front of it, there were three large sage-coloured velour sofas placed in a horseshoe around a large rimu coffee table covered in a thick layer of grey dusty.

"And the guy you got the keys from?" Frank broached.

"The consulate official?"

"Yeah, him. They never said nothin' about Jake to you?"

"No. Should they have?"

"No, no," Frank mumbled breezily, "Just wondering... *Struth!* Is that a split cane Ogden Smith?"

Mounted on the back wall, a couple of rows of antique wooden fishing rods suddenly consumed all of Frank's attention.

"Please have them."

"No, mate, these are worth a bit..."

"Please."

Shaun overrode Frank's prostrations and pointed at the several mounted stuffed rainbow trout that were surrounding the rods.

"As long only as you take these too."

Taking one off the wall, Shaun stopped in his tracks.

In an arc, dotted right across the wood-lined wall were twenty or more neatly filled-in dents.

He pushed it out of his mind. Here he was in this peaceful corner of paradise and all he could think about was bullet spray. He was more damaged by his past than he'd realised. And he needed this place more than he knew. To heal. To start over.

And boy, now he saw it properly, he could see the potential of the place. His mind raced with the possibilities; a fishing retreat, a hotel? He wasn't scared of a bit of graft.

As they wandered around, he saw that the two wings added on to the main house gave four large ensuite bedrooms on each side, in addition to the four bedrooms upstairs in the main body of the lodge. They'd seen better days, but there was furniture in them all, albeit of varying condition. Victorian iron bedsteads, chests of drawers, wardrobes, they were antique and solid, if a little dusty and damp.

Shaun's first assessment had been right. There was a hole in the roof on the right wing, and the rain had gotten into that part of the building causing a fair bit of rot and damage to the rooms. But it was all fixable, Shaun decided as he wandered around, now feeling increasingly pleased with his settlement from Her Majesty's Government.

Leaving Celia busy with her list, the men went outside to explore the barn to the side of the house.

Pulling open the large wooden door, Shaun peered in. The main barn was a large cavernous space. It had been used for stabling and storage.

At the far end of the barn was a wooden partition. It was puzzling. The barn had seemed to extend further from the outside. Shaun absently ran his hand along the joint above him until it hit a bump. It was a peg.

He pulled at it and felt a catch, and then the giving way of a door that opened in his hand.

"Hey, Frank! There's another space behind here."

The ground floor of the room beyond had been used for storage too. There was an ancient bicycle with wobbly-looking wheels, a wheelbarrow, an old push lawnmower, and a full collection of spades, axes and other utensils that would come in quite handy.

"Hey, I've got myself a boat!"

Shaun's eyes were fixed on a Canadian canoe, perfect for pottering on the lake.

"Good-*oh*."

Shaun looked up. Above the storage area was a beam.

It was odd. Why would the beam run across the middle of the barn, like that? Unless...

Grabbing a set of ladders, he carefully placed them against the beam and climbed up.

"What's up there?" Frank called from the bottom, where he was holding the ladders firm.

It was a hidden mezzanine loft.

"A mattress with a quilt."

Shaun swiped the torch on his phone to see more clearly into the shadowy corners.

"And there's a small stove."

"It's a sleepout."

"Maybe."

Shaun climbed back down the ladders. It looked more like a safe room to him. A place to hide.

"Us Kiwis love a bit of camping and extra space for visitors."

Shaun checked himself. There he was again, projecting his damaged mind. Frank was right. It was a sleepout.

They wandered out of the shed.

"What was that?"

Shaun flicked around as he heard it again by the side of the barn.

"What?"

Something moved to the side of Frank, followed by a squawk.

"I don't bloody believe it."

Frank bent down and peered into the thick spiky manuka bush beside the barn.

"It's Rowdy."

"Rowdy?"

"Yeah. Rowdy the Rooster. Gave him to Jake a few years back. Must be getting on a bit by now."

"So, Jake had hens here?"

Frank pointed to the wire netting on an old makeshift compound across the yard.

"Looks like a chook pen to me."

They strolled back towards the house, wandering lazily over to the lakeshore in front of the lounge windows.

"How come a fulla like you lands himself a piece of prime Kiwi real estate, then?"

"It's hardly prime, Frank."

He was making a new start. Frank and Celia were the only friends he had on this side of the world and he didn't want to lie to them, but he couldn't tell them the whole truth either.

"It was a settlement. I did some work and the payment from the British Government was the deeds to this place."

Bending down Frank picked up a stone to skim.

"I guess this may seem like the perfect spot to you. But the reality is, out here's a tough place."

The stone made seven perfect bouncing arcs across the mirrored lake.

"If I were you, I'd sell it and buy a bach at the beach, so's you can go surfin' and have some fun. Not be stuck out here on yer tod."

Shaun contemplated Frank's words as he picked up a flat pebble and then skimmed a perfect seven-bouncer.

Why was Frank so negative about this?

It was so peaceful here. Idyllic even.

Shaun put it down to ignorance. The bloke had probably never travelled. He'd lived here all his life; he didn't realise what a special place it was. And anyway, Shaun didn't think of New Zealand as being particularly lawless, not compared to the places he'd been to. If there was any trouble, he was confident he could soon sort it.

"Nah, the beach's not for me."

Frank sighed.

"I reckoned as much. But, there's things about this pl..."

"Frank! Where've you got to?"

Celia bounded out of the kitchen door, nearly sticking her foot into the hole on the porch decking.

"What's up?" Shaun asked.

Frank went towards her.

"Celia, what you flappin' like an ole chook about?"

"Ah, nothing. I... I got a little freaked out there on my own. I... I heard a noise."

Celia smoothed over her hair with her hand.

"Hope you're not scared of the odd possum?" Frank joked, looking at his wife. "Being out here doesn't suit everyone."

Shaun shrugged.

"*You* like it out here, don't ya?"

"I wouldn't be anywhere else, mate."

"Me either. I can see there's a lot of work needed."

"Yeah. She's a doer-upper, alright."

"And I haven't got anything else to do... Besides, I kinda like it here. It's peaceful."

Frank sniffed.

"Quiet as the grave."

Celia shuddered.

"You'll be needing a builder."

"I can do the work myself."

Frank studied the old lodge resignedly.

"If you need tools, you're welcome to borrow what I've got."

"Thanks, Frank."

"And you'll be staying with us, at least until you can get the electric put on," Celia added.

Shaun studied them both. They'd been so generous and open-hearted. Salt-of-the-earth folk. He'd been lucky to have met them.

"I've burdened you enough. You've both been very kind."

"Ah, no worries."

And that was that. Celia bulldozed all Shaun's protestations.

"By rights, we're neighbours now. And you're gonna need all the help you can get, I reckon."

Frank put his arm around Celia's waist.

"But, what a view, eh?"

"Yeah, you can say that again," Shaun agreed.

It was the first time he'd noticed it. The lake from the house was like a perfect mirror reflecting the rolling volcanic hills covered in the native forest around it.

"It's a special place, alright. And when I'm done, I'll cook you a barbie."

Frank chuckled.

"Now you're talkin' We'll make a Kiwi of you yet."

CHAPTER 6

--------- * ---------

Hugging little Aaron, and then my flatmate Courtney, I fight back the tears.

"You take care, Claire," she whispers to me, her voice catching.

I hoist my backpack over one shoulder. It's so heavy, I wonder how I'm going to cope. Everything I own and need is in this pack.

"Promise to send us some of your lovely photos. I want dolphins, Auntie Claire."

"I've packed my camera, so I'll see what I can do. Be a good boy. I miss you already!"

And with that, I'm out of the door and down the stairs to the high street to wait for my free ride to London with Jac and Annie. They're getting themselves matching tattoos for some loved-up reason that I'm not even going to ask about.

They pull up soon after and I throw the rucksack into the boot. Annie moves to sit in the back with me.

"I can't believe you're finally doing this."

She seems more excited than me.

I'm heading down through France and Italy to Greece. Then over to Crete and the job in a café.

My stomach flips as it dawns on me, I've never been further south than Birmingham.

And to be honest, the scar isn't helping my confidence any. I've been trying to cover the red welt stretching down my neck with scarves and high-neck jumpers, but I know I won't be able to when I'm travelling and the weather's hot.

"Does it look bad?" I ask Annie tentatively.

"Claire, you look great. You always do. Don't worry about the scar. Your hair covers it."

"Thanks, Annie. You always make me feel good."

Perhaps there is such a thing as true love, I consider as I watch Jac and Annie chatting as we drive along.

I curse under my breath as ironically at that moment when I'm thinking about *him* again, The Killers begin blasting Mr Brightside out from the car stereo. *'It was only a kiss.'*

"D'ya think Sion did it?" I ask Annie quietly as we sit in slow-moving traffic on the motorway. We've skirted around this issue before but I've never asked her straight out.

"No."

I'm shocked. She says it so matter-of-factly.

"But the police said…"

Annie squeezes my hand.

"He definitely didn't. The detective was way off beam. My dad hanged himself."

"But… how can you be so sure?"

"Claire, my dad was a man of many layers and plenty of problems. He was really ill, I get that. But he had a mean streak too. That wasn't his illness, it was part of him. A raging, violent temper that the drink brought out. The tattoo I'm getting done on this trip, it's to cover this. See?"

She lifts her loose t-shirt for me to see. There's no mistaking the deep scraped out indentation across her shoulder blade.

"*Shit*, Annie!"

"Belt buckle. It caught me when he was whipping me."

"Why didn't you go to the police?"

"About my dad?"

She shook her head.

"It was complicated."

I get the impression that she's not said much to anyone about this before, apart from Jac who's designed the tattoo that's going to cover it.

She pulls her t-shirt back down and I catch them looking at each other in the rearview mirror.

"I sometimes wonder how different things would've been if I'd've gone with him."

I utter the words half to myself as I stare out of the window at the motorway traffic in the opposite lane. I squash the unwanted feelings of desire that well up deep inside of me when I think about him.

"Never look back," Annie advises wisely, offering me a bottle of water.

"Jase, mate!"

Jac warmly embraces his old army buddy as Annie and I stand behind him on the doorstep of his South London flat.

"This is Annie."

It seems odd meeting Sion's friends.

Jason is tall, dark-haired and like Jac and Sion, he has an air of calm authority about him that puts me immediately at ease.

"And this is Claire."

Jason kisses me on the cheek and I can feel his eyes lingering on my neck as he moves away.

"You're off travelling, I hear?"

"Yes."

I try to keep my voice upbeat but seeing people's reaction pains me more than the cut did.

"I'm on the Eurostar to Paris the day after next. This is my first time in London, so while these two lovebirds are gettin' inked up, I'm gonna make the most of it and be a total tourist."

"Wanna guide?"

"Alright," I answer a little surprised. "That'll be cool."

After a few drinks in Jason's local pub, we've gone back to his flat with a mountain of Chinese takeaway food.

Annie sighs and pushes her bowl away.

"This is my guilty pleasure. I'm not gonna lie, I've eaten way too much of this."

I don't disagree.

"Certainly beats airline grub," Jason agrees, helping himself to another prawn cracker.

I take one too.

"Must be so glamorous, though. Flying everywhere. Seeing new places."

"I see a lot of airports. And airport hotels... Sure, I do get to go to exotic places, but it's not much fun on your own."

"Well, if you ever fly in near where I am, give us a shout."

I colour up.

"Oh God! That sounded awful. I don't mean that in a booty call kinda way. I meant as travel buddies."

"Bet you get plenty of booty call offers from women when you put that airline pilot uniform on," Jac teases.

Thankfully, Jason laughs it off.

"It's okay, Claire. You're not my type anyway."

He gives me a knowing look and I smirk back at him.

Jac doesn't seem to have worked it out, and Jason hasn't told him.

Much later, Annie and I turn in and leave the boys to catch up over a bottle of duty-free whisky that Jason has produced.

But, I can hear every word from the bedroom through the thin plasterboard wall, and I can't help but listen to what they're saying.

"So, what d'ya think?" I can hear Jac say.

"The girls? They're great."

"No. I meant about Sion? Did ya know the truth about him?"

Jason is silent.

All evening, Sion's absence has felt like a presence in their company as they've skirted around what happened. It's only now that they're alone that they begin to talk freely.

"Only me in the dark, then?"

I can hear the tinge of hurt in Jac's voice.

Unable to stop myself, I edge out of bed and open the door.

"He told me too, the night before he went into witness protection. About his work undercover."

They turn around and stare at me standing in the doorway.

"Come and join us," Jac urges. "Wanna dram?"

Dressed in my pyjamas, I shuffle up next to Jac on the sofa.

Between us, Jason and I patch together what we know. In turn, Jac sits there quietly, listening, taking it all in.

Jac bends his head and clinks the ice of his whisky.

"Why didn't he tell me?"

"He wanted a safe place. A bolt hole, where no one would suspect him. That's why you were out of the loop. He only told me the bare minimum too. Said it was safer that way."

"He was right about that," I add, unconsciously touching my neck. "He only came clean with me because he wanted me to go away with him."

"But you stayed?"

"I did."

I take a sip of the peaty whisky.

"I didn't believe him."

Jac stares at me intently.

"Claire? Why? If Sion said he didn't do it, then he didn't do it. He would never lie to you."

"You so sure? After everything you've heard tonight?"

Jason pours us more whisky.

"So you think Sion strung Glyn up and killed him?" Jac mutters, "Never mind the practicalities of that, what was his motive? Why did he do it? Or d'you agree with the detective and think that me and Annie hired Sion to kill her parents so we could inherit the farm?"

"No! 'Course not," I backtrack, horrified. "You'd never do that. Oh, God! Is that what the detective said?"

I can feel my eyes burn and I swallow the hard lump that's forming in my throat.

"But he did do bad shit for a living. He's killed people."

Jac looks away. There's no denying what Sion has done.

"He was undercover, Claire. He was following orders like we all did as soldiers."

I breathe heavily. There's nothing more to say. I'm fully aware of the mistake I've made.

The next day Jason takes me literally everywhere across London. We ride the hop-on-and-off double-decker tourist bus past Buckingham Palace and Hyde Park. It's hot and the gentle breeze blowing onto us as we sit up top in the fresh air is welcomingly refreshing.

Jason's been great company, and I knew straight away that we'd get on.

"What was going on last night?" I ask as we go over the bridge towards Big Ben and the Houses of Parliament. "You've not told Jac you're gay?"

Jason shrugs.

"Jac's never asked. With him farming and me flying, I've not seen him in ages."

"And Sion?"

He's quiet for a bit.

"You gotta remember, Claire, we were in this macho culture."

"Yeah, but there must have been others?"

"Oh God, aye. But we kept it… discreet. Things are changing, but it's never easy to come out, especially in that kinda environment."

We carry on with our tour, making our way over to The Shard where we see all of London stretching out below us from the viewing deck on the seventy-second floor.

"St Paul's looks so tiny."

I've brought my camera along to take some photos but the wind blows my hair across my face and it's too difficult to get a good shot.

"Don't be ashamed of it," Jason says out of the blue.

I lean up against the glass barrier, embarrassed.

"I'm not, it's windy, that's all."

"Think of the scar as a battle wound, Claire."

I try to brush my hair back to cover my neck.

"How did you meet Sion and Jac? 'Cos you were in the RAF, right?"

"Yeah. Helicopter pilot. I flew them out of the sticky messes they'd gotten themselves into. Unless Sion had other ideas, that was."

"What d'ya mean?"

He tells me about an operation where Jason flew them into a village and under heavy gunfire, Sion sprinted across a court-yard and rescued an interpreter.

"Sounds like Sion's pretty fearless?"

"Yeah. He was an amazing soldier. He saved that man's life that day. Claire, I know Sion as well as I know myself, and I'm certain that he'd never kill a civilian in cold blood."

I shiver. The air is cold at this height, even for July.

"Let's go back down," I suggest.

"Alright, how about the Embankment next? The Tate Modern to Westminster?"

I take his arm.

"Can we get an iced coffee?"

After we get back to the flat Jason naps on the sofa like an old man. I've completely thrashed him.

That evening, Jac's mother Callista and her partner Sam come around for supper. Callista lives in London these days, though she's spent lots of time before in Wales.

She's artistic and flamboyant. Her long silver dreadlocked hair is pulled off her face and garnished with dozens of beads. She coos over Jac and Annie's new tattoos, and much to Sam's horror starts discussing getting another one for herself, right across her back.

Of course, Callista's been absolutely everywhere in the world, and by the time we're eating my head is spinning with travel ideas. But I'm starting to feel normal about myself, relaxing in their company.

Until she mentions my scar.

"You don't mind me saying, darling, but that looks very red. What've you been putting on it?"

"Err... I've been covering it with make-up."

"That's no good, sweetie. Manuka honey, that's what you want."

"I'll try it," I answer politely, trying to close down the conversation.

"How did it happen?"

I have the feeling that this is going to happen a lot on my travels and I'm going to need to toughen up, work out strategies to deal with it. On this occasion though, I don't need to. Jac jumps in and answers for me.

"Oh! Claire, that's awful," she exclaims after. "What happened to him?"

"He pleaded guilty to grievous bodily harm so they dropped the attempted murder charge. He got three years. He'll be out in eighteen months."

Another reason to leave.

Cal tuts.

"And what happened to Sion?"

Jason glances at Jac. I can see that he isn't sure if we should be talking about Sion's new identity publicly.

"He's fine. He's gone away for a bit."

Jac swallows a gulp of beer.

"They tried to charge him with murder, Cal. They had me and Annie in for questioning too."

Cal stares at him horrified. She's clearly at a loss for words. For the first time ever.

"Jac's apparently only with me for my money and the farm."

Annie winks at Cal, trying to lighten the mood, but Cal's face has turned a stony-grey and I can tell that it has upset her deeply.

"What?" Sam asks Cal quietly as the table falls silent.

"I'm shocked, that's all," she mutters. "It's worse than living in a fascist state."

"Well, it's all settled now," I tell them. "Sion was free to go."

"But you've still got doubts about Sion?" she asks me, suddenly.

My fork clangs onto my plate, and I mouth an apology and take a drink of my wine. Cal has read my thoughts.

Later, as she gets ready to leave, Cal hugs me tightly, "Bon voyage, darling, you're going to have the most wonderful time."

She whispers in my ear, "You still love him. He didn't kill Glyn. Go find him, sweetie. And then never let him go."

I shake my head. She means well but Sion's gone. Now I need to find myself.

The next day I'm up early, repacking my rucksack, doing last-minute checks.

Jac and Annie come with me to St Pancras to see me off. I hug Annie tightly as we say our goodbyes. In a few hours, I'll be in Paris. My big world adventure is about to begin and I can't wait.

CHAPTER 7

--------✳--------

Shaun sat with Frank in the canoe in the middle of the lake. It was the start of the season and two fishing lines were in the water, but only one was snagging the biting trout, and it wasn't Shaun's.

It was the first time he'd seen the newly painted-up lodge from the water and Frank caught Shaun studying it.

"You'd never think it was the same place. Good on ya, Shaun, ya've done a crackin' job."

The white painted windows popped out of the subtle putty-coloured paintwork, making the lodge look large and homely.

"Yeah. The biggest pain was that hole in the roof, had to re-timber and dry line the rooms. Still a lot of work to do redecorating."

"No pain, no gain, mate. Least ya got the hot water going now."

"I've got Wifi too. And one very noisy rooster that wakes me up at the crack of dawn every morning."

"Rowdy," Frank chuckled. "Celia put her foot down. It was either get rid of that bird or she was putting him in the pot."

"I'm feeding him now, but he's still too fast for me to catch."

Shaun had spent hours trying to coax, cajole and chase Rowdy back into his newly refurbished chicken coop. But Rowdy had a taste for freedom and was not a willing participant. The best he could hope for was to feed him and hope that he'd become more tame. In the meantime, he was getting used to the six a.m. wake-up calls.

Once he was settled, Vern in the hardware store said he'd help him get some layers. He liked the idea of having fresh eggs every morning.

In the space of a month, Shaun had turned the place back into the sumptuous lodge it once was.

But what was he going to do with all those bedrooms? That big barn? And the land?

The place had potential, but he wasn't quite sure for what exactly.

"Can we stop calling it Jake's Place now?"

"Too right. Lake Lodge. That's what ya called it, didn't ya?"

"Yes. Lake Lodge."

The week before, he'd taken a shopping trip to Auckland with Celia.

White goods, electronics, furnishings; he could feel his pulse rising as he tapped in his pin code and felt his bank balance depleting before his eyes. But this place was his forever home. Even if he wanted to, he thought grimly, he could never go back.

Celia, he noticed, clammed up whenever he mentioned Jake. And it was no coincidence. He got a weird look from the folk in town too whenever he mentioned where he was living.

It was obvious that some tragedy had befallen Jake. But he had enough ghosts of his own from Helmand and Syria to deal with, without adding Jake to the collection.

And how could he be spooked, when every morning he watched the spring mists rolling like curls of smoke across the mirrored water?

Celia and a few of their friends and neighbours had arrived by the time Shaun and Frank were back on dry land with a passel of trout.

Shaun had been determined to hold fast to his promise of a barbecue, and Celia had got a group of neighbours together as a housewarming. Everyone was bringing a plate she'd told him and then quickly explained what that meant. Basically, it meant no work for him, apart from the outside table he'd constructed. Soon it was covered in bowls of salads and side dishes his neighbours brought as they arrived. And the smell of charcoal and cooking began to waft across the porch and onto the sandy shoreline below the house.

Frank took over the cooking duties while Celia introduced Shaun to neighbours and friends. The men invited him to go fishing with them, and worryingly after a couple of glasses of pinot, Celia started to take a vocal interest in Shaun's love life. By the end of the evening, she'd promised to fix him up with every single or divorced woman she knew in the town. He wasn't sure how he was going to handle that but he needed to end this new line of interest once Celia had sobered up.

"So, what next?" Frank asked Shaun as they leaned against the island in the newly refurbished kitchen.

Shaun took out his phone and clicked on the contact that the British Consulate had given him.

"I s'pose it's high time I saw about getting a job."

As the evening drew late and everyone had gone home, Shaun relaxed on the sofa in the lounge, alone. Firing up his new games consul onto his new big screen, he loaded his favourite game. It was the same one he used to play online with Jason when he was laid over in some far-flung place and Shaun was in London or on a job.

He couldn't believe it. As he was thinking about Jason, his friend's icon simultaneously flashed up on the screen. Jason was online too.

It was too tempting, and a little drunk he clicked onto messages. Before he thought better of it, he was already connected.

Shaun: Jase? Are you there?
Jason: Hey! Sion? Is that you? How you doing, man?
Shaun: Hi Jase. I'm good
Jason: Great to hear from you. So, you a ghost now?
Shaun: Pretty much

Jason: Where are you?

Shaun considered his answer. The messaging was pretty secure. He was pretty confident that no one would hack his games accounts.

Shaun: Delete this convo after, right?
Jason: Yeah, no worries
Shaun: I'm Shaun Cobain now
Jason: Cobain? As in Nirvana?
Shaun: I'm living in NZ
Jason: North or south?
Shaun: Way up north
Jason: Awesome! Oranges and beaches
Shaun: Something like that.
Jason: I'll come out and see you one day
Shaun: Any time, mate. I've got a place by a lake. Real peaceful. I'm loving it here. How's Jac and everyone?
Jason: They're good. Jac, Annie and Claire came down to London. Claire's great, by the way

Shaun's heart sank.

Shaun: Where's she now?
Jason: She's gone travelling but we're in touch quite often
Shaun: Oh

There was a pause and Shaun could see Jason typing. After a few seconds, the words appeared.

Jason: Not like that, you idiot. That's never gonna happen
Shaun: Sorry, Jase

He should never have thought that. It was an unwritten code. None of his friends would ever move in on another's girl. She wasn't exactly his girl. But it wasn't Jason's style. Thinking about it, Shaun had never met any of Jason's girlfriends.

He smirked to himself, not that the airline pilot would ever be short of female company.

Jason: Claire's gone travelling. She's in Crete for the summer, working in a café. She's messaged me a few times
Shaun: Has she got over the attack?
Jason: It shook her up for a good while, but she's trying to move on with her life
Shaun: Has she said anything about me?

The typing paused. Jason was considering carefully what to say next. Not a good sign, Shaun concluded.

Jason: She really likes you, but she's confused about your past

Shaun rubbed his eyes. He bitterly regretted the last few years, but it was what it was. He couldn't change it.

Shaun: I'm out of all that now
Jason: Hang on in there, mate. I'll talk to her if you like, tell her where you are, see if she'll go see you
Shaun: No, it's too risky. There might be people watching her
Jason: Then, you'll need to think of another way
Shaun: Thanks, Brains. If you have any bright ideas, let me know

Claire still liked him. Shaun thought about nothing else all night.

But how could he reach out to her, get her to come to New Zealand without making her feel like he was entrapping her?

As he lay in the master bedroom in his new king-size bed, the curtains open, he looked out onto the silvery calm moonlit lake and contemplated it some more.

Irish tapped his unlit cigarette angrily against the packet. It was nearing September now and the trail was cold. Even with the huge reward, he'd not had a sniff. Not even a false sighting.

He swiped his phone and looked at the blurry picture that he had of him. It was the only one, a black and white CCTV image looking down from the ceiling into the pub corridor where they'd ambushed him.

He was around six foot in height, athletic. His hair he guessed was a sandy brown, kind of fair but not especially so. His face? There were no discernible features; a straight nose, no scars. Sion Edwards was instantly forgettable.

And that was the problem.

He sparked the lighter and lit his cigarette.

No. The only way to get to him was through the girl.

Claire Edwards had gone travelling. And having a good time, judging by her posts. The Leaning Tower of Pisa, the Trevi fountain in Rome; she'd headed through Italy.

The last two posts she'd put up were a month apart. He studied them carefully. It was the same place. He tapped and re-sized the photo. She was wearing an apron around her waist. On the umbrella in the background, he could make out a name. Cafe Elounda.

He googled the name and found it immediately. It was in Crete.

He scrolled through his phone contacts until he got to Mac O'Shea, an old family friend and sometime buyer, though he'd not worked in England recently.

He was onto a far better thing now. He spent his summers in Greece and his winters in the Caribbean. Not bad for a Bootle boy, Irish thought with some admiration.

Mac was a nimble operator. Every spring he bought his party drugs out of Spain and then spent the summers working the Greek Islands. Moving from resort to resort on his yacht, he dropped the gear discreetly with the young Brits he met in bars, the types who needed to earn a little extra on the side in the clubs, selling pills and powder.

It was working out well for him. No one ever suspected the unassuming leather-skinned Englishman who sat reading British papers in the bar by his anchored yacht.

"Mac? How you doin'? It's Irish... that's right, Connor O'Dwyer... yeah, Irish Eoin's lad.... Yeah, still raining here in Liverpool, you lucky sod... Listen, Mac, are you anywhere near Crete? I need a favour."

"Efharisto."

I thank the Greek couple and take the money they've left on the table for their coffees. Sweeping my hair over my shoulder I cover my neck self-consciously as I clear up after them. The man checks back at me and I can sense that they're talking about my scar.

The days are colder now that it's October and the place has quietened down. Over across from Plaka in the Bay of Elounda, the evening sunlight is catching the island of Spinalonga. It lights up the side of the sandstone fort. Tiny black impenetrable windows pepper the sheer golden walls that sweep into the sea. It's the perfect light for a sensational photograph, it's a shame that my camera's back in my room.

The island was used as a leper colony. Even though it's less than a mile away from the mainland, when the sick people were shipped off there in the rowing boat they never saw their families again.

I take the empty coffee cups to the kitchen and go back out to reset the table. It's been a busy few weeks of work but gazing out at the island every day I find myself thinking more and more of Sion. Where is he now? What's he doing? I wish I could shake myself free of his memory, but I can't.

I video chat to Jason sometimes. He's keeping mad hours, flying in and out of Singapore. When I tell him I've been thinking about Sion, he gives me a strange look.

Don't let the past control the future, he says to me. See things as they are now and let yourself make a fresh start.

I've thought about that a lot. And I agree with Jason. I need to move on.

CHAPTER 8

---------✳---------

Shaun felt about twelve years old as he sat waiting outside the School Principal's office.

The secretary had smiled kindly at him and asked him if he wanted a cup of tea when he arrived, but Shaun had been far too nervous to accept.

This was ridiculous, he told himself. He'd got himself and five of his men out of a fox hole covered by enemy snipers in Afghanistan. In Iraq, he'd coolly broken into a desert compound and rescued two journalists about to be beheaded by Isis jihadis, and yet here he was sitting outside a headteacher's office and he was a total wreck.

He put it down to his past. School had never been a happy place for him. So why had he bothered coming?

When he'd called, the secretary had told him that school was rural, and she wasn't lying. It had taken him a good hour in his car to reach this place, far up in the north on the other side of the vast kauri forests.

And truth be told, when he arrived he very nearly hadn't got out of the car. But then, he'd seen the school, perched above the pristine sands in the bay. Carved totem poles were dotted around the front, and alongside the school sat an intricately-carved wooden house which made him curious. It didn't look like any school he'd ever been to before.

"Mr Cobain, good to meet you at last."

A tall, olive-skinned man took his hand and shook it firmly.

"I'm John. John Kara, the principal.

Shaun had been practising pronouncing the greeting in the car.

"Kia Ora, John. I'm Shaun."

John Kara's face cracked into a broad smile.

"Kia Ora."

He guided Shaun through to his office, an unassuming space with walls covered in photographs of students. Sports teams, dramas, boys and girls in traditional dress.

Fastening himself behind his desk, the principal scanned through the printed email on his desk.

"So… back in July, we agreed with the Ministry that you could fill our classroom assistant vacancy. Bit unusual, but they gave us your paperwork and asked us to do them a favour."

Shaun nodded a little sheepishly. He had instantly got a warm feeling about John Kara, but there was no denying it, it was now October. He'd left it very late to get this job.

"Yeah, well. We're usually struggling to get staff up here, but the thing is, Shaun," he said, looking up from the paper, "A teacher who used to work here, they moved back home and so I'm afraid we've filled the space."

"Oh…Well…"

Shaun got up to leave, stretching his hand towards the principal.

"I'm sorry to have taken your time."

"Hold up, a second."

The headteacher regarded him quizzically.

"You've come out all this way to see us. Fancy a look 'round? See what we do here?"

Shaun relaxed.

"I'd love to."

"Good on ya."

"Can I ask you about the carved poles and that red-wood building outside?"

"I can do better than that. I can show you," John said, grabbing his keys off the desk and ushering Shaun out of the office.

"So, this is our marae. It's where we teach our kids about Māori culture."

Shaun copied the headteacher and slipped his trainers off to go inside the intricately carved building he'd admired.

"It feels like a church."

"Yeah. It's a sacred space. We use it for ceremonies as well as teaching. Come outside and I'll show you what else we're doing."

Shaun followed the principal as he took him around the back of the marae to what looked like a large porch. But under which a long wooden canoe rested on a scaffolded base.

Two adolescent boys were hard at work carefully chiselling into the wood on the prow.

Shaun couldn't help but run his hand over the intricate carvings.

"Did you guys do this?"

One of the two boys gave him a shrug.

"Yeah, me and a few others."

"Well, you have some talent, my friend. This is awesome."

The principal noticed the boy's shoulders rising slightly and his mouth curling at the edges as Shaun studied the carvings closely.

"Have you tried her in the water yet?"

Shaun looked up, his fingers still caressing the wood.

"Nah, you gotta carve her first," the boy answered casually, "D'ya wanna come and see it when we put her in?"

Shaun grinned.

"You bet I do. I've never seen anything like it. How many are you planning to put in the boat?"

"The waka," the boy corrected him.

"Waka? Did I say that right?"

The boy nodded.

"We're gonna start with ten and see."

"Good to see ya here; Rawiri, Matthew," the principal jumped in. "You two had your lunch yet?"

The boys mumbled that they had.

"Okay. Well, make sure you get some fresh air and a bit of a relax before you go back into class."

He turned back to Shaun and they walked the length of the ten-metre canoe.

"It's a project that some of our more energetic boys and girls are doing at the moment. Some of the kids, like Rawiri, here," he whispered to Shaun, "We couldn't get them to come to school before, and now they're here all the time."

"He's a great kid."

Shaun glanced over at the two boys who were back concentrating on their carving.

"Rawiri pretty much sounds like me at school. Honestly, I'm not sure if I'd've made a good classroom assistant, I didn't go to school myself that often."

John paused and studied the waka carefully.

"What changed you?"

"The army. I was in for ten years."

"Did you see active duty?"

Shaun nodded.

"Plenty."

"Believe me, Shaun, guys like you are usually the best types. We want people who'll learn with them. Take an interest in them, inspire them. Help them to structure themselves and empower them to find their way in the world."

Shaun looked back at the boys as they left the waka.

"I wish I'd had a project like this at school."

It was lunchtime, the air was warm and dry. The teachers and youngsters were wearing short-sleeved shirts.

Walking around, his eyes lingered on a furious game of touch rugby over on the playing field.

"They're fast," Shaun observed out loud as he paused to watch them play. "They'd be good too if their passes weren't all going forward."

"Fancy yourself as a bit of a coach d'ya?" John joked.

"Nah. Being Welsh we're all rugby crazy."

The principal clapped as a player broke out and ran in a try, touching the ball down between two bags set up as posts.

"You still want a job?"

"Yeah, but as I said, I don't think I'm qualified."

"I do have something. It's only temporary, but I have a feeling about you. Our school hostel's closing at the end of the term because the numbers have dropped too low. Ari, our hostel manager, his wife's having a baby in a few weeks. So, I want to help him out if I can."

"What does it involve?"

"Staying here for two months. Making sure that the five boys staying in the hostel are fed, do their studying and go to bed, basically. And you'll probably be roped into the odd game of rugby if you're up to it?"

Shaun chuckled.

"Think I can handle that. What happens on weekends?"

"The kids go home Friday after school and come back Sunday evening."

Shaun thought it through. He didn't have anything else to do.

"I don't know much about kids."

"Don't worry. You'll learn fast. And Ari'll be around."

"Alright. I'll do it."

"Fantastic. I've got your paperwork and checks. Can you start Sunday night?"

It was Shaun's last evening at the lake. He was sad to be going, but being honest he needed human interaction too. It was so quiet at the lake.

According to Vern in the hardware store, there were camps in the forest, illegal marijuana plantations run by hardcore criminal gangs. Right now, he'd be happy to say hi to anyone, even a Hell's Angel. He'd always been independent, but out here he'd never felt so utterly alone.

He gave Frank a call and let him know that he'd be gone for a few weeks, in case they thought that he'd suffered the same ending as Jake. Whatever that was.

He'd filled the feeder to the brim for Rowdy, but seeing as the rooster had lived on his own all these years just fine without him, he wasn't too concerned.

Afterwards, he got his bag from the built-in wardrobe and began to pack his clothes. It was starting to warm up now and he was packing mainly shorts and t-shirts. Remembering Frank's advice, he searched for the Tilley hat. He'd put it up on the top shelf of the wardrobe.

His hand scraped the empty shelf. He was certain he put it there.

Grabbing a chair, he climbed up to eye level to try and find it. There it was, right at the back.

Stretching his arm into the top space he located the cloth hat, and then oddly his fingers scraped a hard metal corner. There was something else up there too.

He stretched his hand out and angled it around the rectangular-shaped metal, nudging the object towards him until he could see it properly. It was an old biscuit tin.

Opening it up, he found a collection of sepia-coloured newspaper clippings. Photographs of schoolboys in their sports teams and the same young man in a singlet top and shorts, holding a trophy. And below each photograph, in the caption, was a reference to Jake Saunders.

Buried underneath the cuttings lay a desk diary, embossed 2017. That was only three years ago. Shaun examined it curiously. That meant that Jake was around more recently than he thought? More recently than he'd been led to believe.

He opened the book.

The first few pages were covered in scrawled handwriting and the rest of it was blank. Jake had tried to start writing a diary but had given up after a few days.

He placed the diary in his suitcase, there'd be plenty of time to read it at the hostel.

It was late but he wasn't tired, so he fired up the games consul to see if Jason was online. It had become a dangerous habit. But especially at night, on his own, it felt like he was hanging off the cliff-face in mid-air again. And the messaging between him and Jason was the only thread left to who he really was. Talking to Jason was like talking to family. His only family.

Jason: Hey, man. Are you there?
Shaun: Yes. Where are you?
Jason: In London. I'm off for a week
Shaun: Out last night then?
Jason: Yes, I was.
Shaun: Meet anyone?
Jason: Maybe.
Shaun: Was she fit?

The conversation stalled for a minute and Shaun saw the dots on the screen where Jason was typing. At last, the words appeared.

Jason:... He was

Shaun stared at the screen. Was it a typo?

Shaun: He! Lol. You coming out on me, bro?

At last, a response.

Jason: Yes

Holy crap! He was.
How had he missed that?
Family. Who was he trying to kid? How well did he even know his best friend?
He stared at the screen. He needed to respond, and fast.

Shaun: Look, Jase mate, I'm a bit shocked, that's all. 'Cos you've never said or even hinted that you were gay. But I'm pleased you've told me, and I wish I was there with you right now having a beer
Jason: Yeah. But easier this way

His stomach lurched with awakening guilt. All those times

he'd teased him about his job.

Shaun: Shit man! I'm sorry for all the air hostess jokes
Jason: No worries. FYI they're called cabin crew now

Shaun cringed.

Jason: But you were half right. My last boyfriend was a flight attend-
ant
Shaun: How did I miss this?
Jason: I wasn't exactly shouting about it

He wasn't the best with emotions, saying stuff. He knew Jason stuck to the usual topics too: football, beer, going out, work, gaming. And now he knew why.
No, he needed to tell him.

Shaun: Jase, you're like a brother to me. I'll always be there for you

A pause and Shaun held his breath. Had he said too much?

Jason: Yeah, you to me too.

The typing started again.

Jason: You thought more about Claire?

Shaun breathed a deep sigh. They were going deep again. Should he tell Jason that he had thought about pretty much nothing else for the last week?
He'd cooked up a hare-brained plan but it could backfire badly, especially if Claire still thought he was a dangerous killer.

Shaun: I need to run something by you. Here's the link

Shaun had set up a webpage with photos of the newly painted lodge. Alongside it was an advert.
Jason typed the link into his phone.

Jason: Is this where you're living? It's stunning
Shaun: I live right on the lake
Jason: Can I apply?

Shaun: Unfortunately not. There's only one person I'm accepting for this job

Shaun reread what he had written as he waited for a reaction from his friend. Reading it again, he hoped it didn't sound too cheesy or too obvious that it was him.

'Enthusiastic all-rounder needed to help transform a large lakeside house into a hotel.

Duties will include decorating and preparing the rooms for the season and helping to run the hotel when the guests arrive.

The successful candidate must have experience in the hospitality industry and excellent customer service skills.

The owner will be away until December, and so anyone applying for this job will need to be happy to work independently and living alone in a remote but stunning location.

For more information contact shaun.cobain@.....'

Jason: Great idea. Let me know when you're ready to share it and I'll get Claire to apply

Shaun: How will she react? Will she be mad?

Jason: What've you got to lose, mate?

Shaun: She might think it's a trap and I'm some nut job stalker or killer? Or both

Jason: There is that. But me and Jac vouched for you. Told her what you were really like. For some reason, after we told her all about your sordid past, your monster nights and all those dodgy women you went with, we still haven't managed to scare her off.

Shaun: Great!

Jason: Only kidding. NZ's on her list, her dad's from there. I'm sure she'll jump at the chance of a job

He was right. He knew that Claire was headed this way on her travels to find out more about the name on her birth certificate.

Jason was gay. He didn't underestimate what a big deal that was for him to come out like that. So, why then did the fact he knew about Claire's search for her father send a wave of jealousy crashing through him?

God! He missed talking to her.

They used to chat to each other every day. And although they'd only had one date, a walk along the estuary to the beach, he still felt that she was his. And they'd kissed in the car once too. It was after he'd told her everything and had asked her to come here with him. He'd sensed her confusion, even then.

Of course, the next day things quickly spiralled out of control. And in a few short hours, she'd been attacked, and he'd been arrested for murder. How on earth was he going to turn that around?

And if she did accept the job, how was he going to stop her running for her life when she found out that he was her boss?

The man she believed to be a cold-blooded killer. The man who'd fallen in love with her.

CHAPTER 9

--------*--------

The man's been hanging around the café for three days.

On the first evening, he ordered gyros and a large beer and sat for two hours reading a British newspaper. I chatted to him a little once I managed to settle myself. Hearing that Liverpudlian lilt in his voice filled me at first with panic. My brush with the Scousers still makes me nervous, which is ridiculous considering well over half a million people share the same accent. This chap tells me that he owns a yacht in the marina and is passing through.

The same man comes to the café again late the following lunchtime. And this time, I have a longer chat with him. His name's Mac. He's retired, divorced and spends every summer on his boat. Nice for some. I get him a Greek salad and a plate of sardines cooked in garlic and oregano.

As he's finishing his meal, a young man joins him at the table. He looks around before sitting down and appears a little startled when I come over.

He orders a small beer. Judging by his accent he's British too, but southern. London. if I had to guess, though I'm no expert.

The young man keeps looking my way. So, I go up and ask him if he wants to order food. But he clears his throat and shakes his head. It's odd, I'm not often wrong about people trying to attract my attention.

After he's finished his beer, the young man leaves. But I see him again in the late afternoon. He's hanging around by my accommodation, smoking a roll-up as I leave and rush down to the café.

After I finish the evening shift I see him again. He's sitting in a bar up the street with another man and he looks my way as I walk past. I give him a smile of acknowledgement. It's nothing unusual, Plaki's a small place. After a while, you come to recognise people. But the way he looks at me unnerves me, and I carry on walking a little quicker.

A couple of minutes later I sense someone behind me. The street is quiet away from the main drag. I listen as I walk, slowing down a little. I'm not imagining it. Even though the street is deserted the footsteps behind me are still there.

At the next junction I turn sharply. It's away from my room but I want to be sure it's not my imagination. I speed up. The scraping of feet behind me continues, faster.

I freeze. Then spin sharply. Around fifty metres behind me, slunk into the shadows of a door and scrambling in his pocket for a packet of cigarettes, is that young man again.

I turn back towards him.

"Are you following me?"

"Uh… no."

He looks sheepishly at me, before putting on a fixed overly-confident smile.

"What you doing here, then?"

I'm trying my best to be assertive but inside I'm all jelly.

"So… maybe… I wanted to see you? We could have some fun. You and me."

He's bullshitting. I can tell.

"That's never gonna happen. Leave me alone."

I walk back past him, marching away swiftly until I'm back again at the street corner, and when he's out of sight I sprint back to my digs.

I'm used to drunk tourists and come-ons. This wasn't like that. I'm not sure if it's post-traumatic after the assault like Annie suggested, but it's rattled me.

The next morning when I wake, he's there again. This time, drinking a coffee from a paper cup, sitting on the step of a closed-up takeaway a hundred metres down the road in the morning sunshine. He's playing it cool but I can see him taking frequent glances this way, up at my window.

It can't be a coincidence I tell myself, pulling back from the window. I'm positive now that he's stalking me so I get my camera out and focus it on his face, taking a shot of him. I'm not too sure why but it makes me feel that I'm doing something about him.

It's the third day in a row that Mac comes back to Café Elounda. It's certainly not because of my charms. He spent most of the previous afternoon sitting alone reading the paper.

"Back again?" I ask him chipperly.

It's Friday evening and the place is full. He's squeezed up against two large Greek men on a small table looking out towards Spinalonga Island.

"On your own tonight?"

"Err... yeah, I am."

"You alright squished up there? I've got a table inside if you prefer."

"No, it'll be fine, love. Besides, I've got a cracking view of the leper colony."

I wink at him.

"If y' misbehave we'll send you over there in yer boat,"

His face changes. Gone's the good-humoured, bantering tourist. The jaw of his stony face is hard-set and he pierces me with his icy-blue eyes.

"That's what happens then, is it chuck? When people do something they shouldn't?"

I freeze. I can feel the blood draining from me.

"Like grassing up the people they work for? Who pay them good money to do a job."

His voice takes on a menacing edge.

"They get sent somewhere far away?"

My lungs feel like they're deflating and I'm struggling to

breathe.

"I'm not sure what you mean."

Mac motions his head towards the island.

"That place. A hundred years ago, if you got sent there, it might as well've been the other side of the world. Goes to show ya. Distance, like everything, it's a matter of perspective... And a matter of time. Don't ya agree?"

His eyes bore into me as I squirm.

"That's a nasty cut you've had there, love."

I recoil, desperately wanting to bolt, but I'm hemmed into the space between the tables by the large Greek who's shifted further back in his seat.

"You're one of them," I finally manage to gasp, terrified. "One of the Scousers."

His skinny brown fingers grab onto my hand, squeezing it tightly so I can't get it free and can't leave.

"You got a bit damaged last time. But you've still got a very pretty face. D'you know what a Birkenhead smile is?"

"What d'you want from me?"

"We take a knife and we cut..."

Trying to wriggle free of his hand, I knock against the big Greek behind me, trying to attract the attention of the table next to us. But the big Greek guy is in the middle of a story and everyone is laughing at him, oblivious to my distress.

"As I was saying," he grips me tighter. "We cut with the knife. From the corner of each mouth up to the ear. Put a big grin on ya face forever. No one'll notice your neck, after that."

"Let me go."

I manage to raise my voice a little to him, though it comes out as a croak.

A young Greek woman at the next table thankfully turns around and nudges her boyfriend. They're both looking our way now, obviously noticing my distress.

Mac releases my hand but pushes a business card into it. I instantly drop it into my apron pocket, like it's burnt me.

He stands up to leave and the young couple look away.

"Gonna try somewhere else tonight. Bit chocka out here."

I retreat as quickly as I can, but he follows me squeezing nimbly through the crammed table space.

Then, from nowhere he's facing me again. And I'm cornered against a patio heater. I try not to freak out. No one's probably paying any attention to me. It's massively busy here. He's standing facing me now, his cold eyes drilling into mine once more.

"If you hear from Sion Edwards, give us a call and I promise you won't get hurt. Otherwise…"

His finger brushes along my cheeks, tracing a wide arc across my face from ear to ear.

"Use that pretty head of yours, Claire," he says under his breath to me, nodding towards the island.

"And remember, chuck, these days there's nowhere safe to hide."

It takes me ten minutes to stop shaking. As I stand in the toilet looking into the mirror over the sink, I can hear the boss calling. They're too busy for me to slope off, but I can't go out. Not like this.

He shouts through the door.

"Claire? Get your ass out here. There's tables to get food to."

"Sorry, Boss," I answer, still quaking. "I'll be there right away. I'm not feeling well. I've got a migraine."

"Me too. From all the complaining customers. Now get here and get going."

I inhale deeply. Mac has gone. Dropping his card into the bin full of dirty toilet paper feels cathartic. He's said his piece.

I dry my hands and emerge from the bathroom. Ducking my head, I refasten my apron. It's a busy shift. Smile, serve, clear, repeat. It's all I need to do.

Chanting that mantra in my head, I flash a smile at the boss, grab a tray of drinks from the bar and take it over to the waiting table.

I work on auto-pilot for the rest of the evening, smiling and serving until the last table's cleared.

"What's goin' on with you tonight?"

It's the boss again, Christos.

"Nothing.".

"Don't give me that crap. It was that old English man. He upset you."

I shrug, but suddenly from somewhere deep down it's too much and the tears begin to flow.

"Shit. I'm so sorry, Christos."

He puts his arm around me and sits me down at the bar inside. Pouring us both an ouzo he sits next to me on a barstool.

"Tell me, Claire. What's up?"

"There was this guy, back home. We used to chat when I worked the bar. We got to be good friends. I liked him, Christos. Anyway, turns out he's in trouble. Big trouble with some seriously bad guys."

I fill him in on how I got the scar and the conversation with Mac. I even mention the young man who followed me.

"I'm sure they're watching my moves."

"You have to get out of here."

"How?"

"Claire, you've been a big help to me here. Leave it with Christos. It's the end of the season. I'll sort you out."

He walks me back to my rented accommodation, a room in his aunt's house and chats to her by the front step while I retrieve my camera and send Christos my shot of the stalker boy.

She pats my shoulder as I move past her to my room. Even though she doesn't have a word of English or me of Greek, her touch tells me that she's looking out for me and I disappear gratefully up the stairs.

Later, looking out of the window I see a movement in the street. I switch off the lights and crouch down, peeping out from under the window.

It's the young man again and he's looking up towards my room. I'm certain now that Mac has paid him to keep an eye on me.

It's after midnight and I'm not sure what time-zone Jason's in. I try calling him but there's no response. He's probably overhead somewhere in the skies.

In the end, I send him a text.

Jason, I need your help. Call me when you can. The Scousers sent someone to try and get me to tell them where Sion is. And I'm being followed. They haven't given up. I'm scared.

An email landed into Shaun's new account. He'd only created it for Claire so he was a little surprised.

'*Check our channel.*'

Shaun raced into the living room and fired up the games consul.

Jason: Claire sent me a message. She's working in a restaurant in Crete. The Scousers sent a man there. He threatened her, tried to get her to tell them where you are. She's going out of her mind. How do you want to play this?

Shaun leaned back from his laptop and rubbed his eyes. This was bad. He clicked onto his advert page. It was a little rough but he didn't have a choice. He had to put his plan into action.

Shaun: Hi Jase, Tell her that her social media accounts are being watched. She needs to stop posting where she is. Send her the job details. We'll need to get her out of there. Whatever you do, don't tell her it's me. It's not safe for her to know.'

Since our conversation, Mac hasn't been back to the café and both Christos and I have come to the conclusion that the Scousers are a bit desperate.

Christos has found out that the young man with Mac is working the summer as a chugger, getting tourists off the street to dine in one of the restaurants up the road.

As of yesterday he's unemployed Christos tells me, and somehow his accommodation has also become double booked. He's been told to move on from Plaka. That's how it works around here. Everyone's related to everyone some way or other and they all help each other out.

I click open the message from Jason. We're only using texts now I've found out they're watching my social media posts. It's made me a little paranoid, still, perhaps I can turn that to my advantage?

Jason's message blows my mind. I knew he had some jet-setting friends but this is amazing. It's a job opportunity. In New Zealand.

I click on the link and wait impatiently for it to load. And I'm not disappointed when it does. The photographs are of a large coffee-coloured wooden mansion on the shoreline of a lake. In front of the house is the whitest of sandy beaches and to the side are ferns the size of trees. The waters of the lake reflect the forest around it. It looks lush and tropical. Remote and wild.

Inside, the pictures show a state-of-the-art kitchen and a large living area that looks out onto the lake.

I picture myself standing by the shore. I've always wanted to go to New Zealand. It's been a dream since I was a kid to find the father that I've never known. At last, this is my chance.

Excitedly I skim-read the advert. Am I what they're looking for?

'Enthusiastic'? I can certainly be that. An 'allrounder'? What does that even mean? I'll give anything a go, even painting though I've never held a paintbrush in my life.

Jason says it's a friend of a friend who has to go away so needs someone to get the place ready for guests, and then needs help running it.

To me it sounds like fate.

And what do I have to lose? I need to get away from Greece now they've found me.

It takes me almost an hour to draft my enquiry, and by the end I'm running late for work. Everything I write about myself sounds so clunky and lame. So I finally plump for a simple email. If the employer wants more information, he can ask me or arrange a call.

Dear Mr Cobain,

I would love to come and help get your Lake Lodge ready for guests. I am the enthusiastic allrounder you are looking for. I'm a waitress and a bartender and am free for the next six months so I can start straight away.
Please let me know if you would like any more information.

Best wishes,
Claire Williams

I check my sent folder. It's gone.

Shaun Cobain. It's odd thinking of another person called Sion. His name is spelt differently, of course, but it still feels like a good omen especially because he also has the coolest surname in the world.

I quickly dismiss the fantasy of Shaun Cobain as the great Kurt's cousin. And anyway, the mysterious Mr Cobain probably won't even reply. There are bound to be hundreds of applicants, thousands even, applying for a cool job like this one. I try to dampen my hopes and dreams. This is another hook in the ocean. I probably won't get a bite.

After my shift, I sit and have a drink with Christos and it's quite late the next morning when I finally get around to checking my emails.

There, in my inbox is a new message. Nervously, I open it.

'Dear Ms Williams,

I am pleased to say that I would like to offer you the position of being

my 'enthusiastic allrounder.'
  I will be in touch.

> *Kindest regards,*
> *Shaun Cobain.'*

Yes! I read it again and then fist punch the air. Yes!
I've got it.
Things are finally working out for me. My dreams have come true. I'm going to New Zealand.

CHAPTER 10

----------✳︎----------

"What d'ya mean she left five days ago? She's been posting up feckin' piccies of herself with her buddies in Crete every day for the last week?"

Mac could hear Connor O'Dwyer's voice rising as he sat back into the cream leather sofa seat on his yacht.

He'd reached his winter mooring in Lefkada, tucked anonymously away between the hundreds of other boats in this vast marina. In a week he'd be resting up in St Kitts where he'd be drinking rum punches until next spring.

He'd been putting off the call.

He knew how volatile Irish could be, and even though he was safely out of the way, he didn't want to get on the wrong side of the Scousers, particularly Irish. And besides which, Mac quite liked his ears. How else would he keep his sunglasses on his head, he joked to himself.

"She had help."

Mac tried to speak calmly as he filled O'Dwyer in.

"Her Greek boss ran my boy out of town and then they got her off the island. She's probably in Athens or even out of the country by now."

"*Bollocks!*"

Mac heard something smash.

"Sorry, Irish. She's had a card with a number to call, and I proper put the frighteners on her."

There was silence at the other end.

"Look, Connor, lad. I've been in this game long enough to know who's a player, and who's not. And she's not one. Without a word of a lie, she went white as a sheet when I mentioned this Sion fella."

Irish was still quiet. That wasn't good.

Mac started again.

"I think the slash to her neck did the trick. She's on the run but she's not running to him. Why else would she be doin' a summer here?"

"Thanks, Mac."

His voice was quiet, and much to Mac's relief he sounded more level.

"We good, Irish?"

"Sure. I'll be sending you a little something for your troubles."

"That's very much appreciated."

"She's a dead-end, Irish. I'm sure."

The little Northland community way up on the Hokianga Peninsula was certainly feeling the sunny Sunday vibe as Shaun strolled along the beach.

There were a couple of youngsters out surfing in the bay, some kids were sand sledging in the dunes. Three men in singlet vests and shorts were fishing off the rocks and enjoying the sun, the fresh sea air and a couple of cold ones.

Still, even though there were people around, the place retained a wildness about it. Perhaps it was the lack of population up here, but there was something about the place that still felt untamed. Authentic. It fascinated him.

He'd been delaying going to the hostel for as long as he could. He'd kicked around the place, wandering along the beach and dunes for a good hour before he turned to head back to his car. The job had seemed like a good idea last week, but since then so much had happened.

Claire was coming.

That was all he'd been able to think about.

He'd sorted her tickets out for her and she was arriving on Wednesday. Celia and Frank had kindly offered to pick her up from the airport.

He'd spent the last few days frantically getting everything ready so that she'd be comfortable living in the lodge on her own.

He hadn't told anyone that he knew Claire. It was better that way. As far as they were concerned she was employed via the internet as a house-sitter for him, getting the place ready for guests.

It felt right having her here.

Jason had filled him in on Claire's brush with the Scousers again, and with Jason's guidance (and airline staff discount code) he'd bought her three separate flights.

The first was to Singapore where she'd do an overnight layover. The next day she had a flight to Kuala Lumpur where she would change airlines and fly the last leg out to Auckland. Jason was confident, with those moves there was no easy way she'd be traced.

And once she got here, she'd be safe at the lake with him. He'd make sure of that.

Back in the car and unable to put it off any longer, Shaun made his way up to the car park by the side of the school hostel.

Grabbing his bag, he sauntered to the door where a huge Māori man in shorts and the biggest t-shirt Shaun had ever seen came out to greet him.

He was used to big, muscular men in the army, but this guy was on another level. He was literally a man mountain.

"Ari?"

Shaun held out his hand.

"Hey, Kia Ora, bro. Shaun, right?"

"Yeah."

Ari took his hand and then surprised Shaun with a hug that only a bear could muster. Not many men could make Shaun feel tiny.

"Don't be standin' there, come on in."

Shaun, taking his cue left his trainers by the row of footwear lining the porch and followed him inside the school hostel.

Ari ushered Shaun into the large kitchen. In the centre was a table with eight wooden chairs, and off from the kitchen was a television room with sofas and colourful bean bags lying around. The last public room on the ground floor was lined with shelves of books, and along the far wall there was a fitted bench with desktop computers and a printer.

"Study area?" Shaun guessed.

Ari smiled.

"Not used as much as the television room."

He pointed at the door beyond.

"Through there's the staff dormitory. I'll show you. They use it for teachers who move up here and don't have accommodation. But at the moment it's just you and me."

Shaun went through and Ari opened one of the dormitory doors for him.

"This is a great resource for the school, it's a shame they're closing it. What you going to do?"

Ari shrugged.

"Don't worry, it's gonna be full-on for me with the baby."

"I heard," Shaun grinned. "Congratulations."

"Yeah. And after Christmas, I'm starting my teaching course. I'm lovin' workin' with these guys and Mr Kara says he'll give me a placement."

"That's awesome. What subject?"

"Māori studies."

"So… are you the guy doing the big boat?"

"The waka? Yeah, man. Did you see it?"

"Did I see it? It's awesome!"

"Ah yeah. It will be when it's done."

"Can I help?"

"Sure, bro. We can do with all the help we can get, eh."

"Cool."

A truck pulled up outside.

Ari glanced out of the window.

"Our first lodger back from the weekend. That's Rawiri."

Shaun saw the young man bolting from the truck with a sports bag and rucksack. The boy ducked his head as the female voice called after him from the car.

"Call me this week, yeah?"

Without turning, he gave her a farewell salute and headed straight into the house. Shaun heard the fourteen-year old's footsteps drum up the wooden stairs, presumably into his room upstairs.

"I met Rawiri working on the waka. He seems happy to be back."

"Yeah, he's a livewire, that one. His mum's lives out in the wops. It's a two hour round trip for them twice a week. Didn't use to have much luck getting him here, but since the waka he's back after every weekend."

Over the next two hours he was introduced to all of the five boys.

In addition to Rawiri, there were twelve-year-old twins whose parents were dairy farmers way up north. The hostel was a home from home for them too, and they dumped their things in their rooms in record time, racing down to play on the games consul in the living room. Noah, a quiet seventeen-year-old, joined them a short while later with Mateo, another older boy. He raised an eyebrow towards Shaun.

"Who's the Pom, eh?"

Ari bristled.

"This is Shaun. He'll be staying here, helping me. In case the baby comes in the night and I have to go to the hospital with Michelle."

"Good to meet you."

Shaun extended his hand. Mateo stood motionless. He was easily the largest school student there. Six four and broad.

"I'm eighteen. We don't need no Pākehā babysitter."

"We're not going into this now, Mateo," Ari batted back breezily. "Principal Kara has kindly employed Shaun to help me out. And that means I get to spend a little time with Michelle and the baby when he or she makes an appearance."

"What's Pākehā?" Shaun asked quietly.

Ari's eyes met his.

"White man."

"Oh."

"Don't stress. He'll come 'round. And we'll soon whip ya into shape. Get rid of that Pommy accent of yours and have ya talkin' like a Kiwi."

Mateo made a small huffing sound as Ari started recounting his trauma of assembling the new cot he'd bought the day before.

"What's Mateo's problem? Is it me?" Shaun asked once he and Ari were alone in the kitchen again.

"Ah, ignore that. He likes to think that he's my right-hand man."

Ari went over to the fridge.

"So, now everyone's here, we'll get the show on the road, eh? And get these snags on the barbie."

"Snags?"

"Yeah, man. Sunday sausage sizzle."

Ari laughed at Shaun's mystified face and handed him a bag of onions to peel and slice.

"Welcome to New Zealand, my friend,"

It was after ten when Shaun finally had a moment to himself. The boys were all in their rooms, but not before they'd consumed a mountain of sausage and fried onion sandwiches, run off afterwards with a good hour of touch rugby.

Shaun had piled in and Rawiri had run the socks off him, but even Ari admitted he wasn't bad for a Pom. Mateo even grudgingly started passing Shaun the ball.

He lay back on his single bed. The place might be on a different continent and in a different context, but hostel living was familiar ground after the years in social care and then the army. He liked it here he decided, closing his eyes. Ari was generous and welcoming, and they were a good bunch of boys.

In a couple of days Claire would be arriving at the Lake Lodge. She'd be starting her journey soon. He tried to block it from his mind but his stomach churned at the thought that she would be near him again.

He'd bought a ute for her to use before he left. It was nothing fancy, but it would mean that she could drive safely over the rough tracks to town when she needed supplies.

He reached for his phone and texted her. He couldn't help it, his heart pounded when he pictured her reading it.

He *so* needed to get a grip.

'Have a good flight. Shaun'

He stretched over and reached for Jake's diary in his bag.

'Jake Saunders' was written carefully in capitals on the inside of the front cover. Inside, the writing was spidery but easy to read once he got used to it.

The first entry under January 1st was dated January 7th. And seeing as there were only a couple of entries in the whole book, Jake hadn't been much of a diarist. He'd given up writing before the end of the first month. Still, Shaun was curious. What was Jake's life at the lodge like?

January 7th

'Mikey McCloud at the station asked me to keep this diary since the last comings and goings. It's evidence, Mikey says. If you're not me reading this, forgive the spellings and bad grammar. I'm no scholar.'

Shaun smiled. Neither was he.

'After Constable Harris drove up to the camp in the forestry, I've not seen hide nor hair of those Cobras thugs.

Been a peachy New Year week and the lake's been buzzing. Some kids up from town camped New Year's Eve and did a fair bit of boozing, letting off a bit of steam. They were good kids though. Cleaned up after themselves before they left. I'd give my eye teeth to be that age again. There's been a lot of boats out on the lake and a fair few families up here in the daytime, swimming and having picnics.

Been into town for supplies today. Got me some feed for the chooks and enough groceries to last a couple of weeks, now I'm getting new visitors staying with me.

Rowdy, the rooster's still playing up. Wish I never agreed to have him off Frank. He's a rum bird that one, alright. I'm sure Frank passed him off to me so as he could get a lie-in. The so-and-so's waking me up at six every morning. And the worst of it is that I can't bloody catch the little blighter to take him back.

Frank's pesky rooster, Shaun chuckled. Some things hadn't changed. But who were the Cobras?

The snake sprayed on the boarded-up door was a cobra too. Was the graffiti marking their territory? How long had it been there?

He put Jake's diary down onto the floor by the bed. Jake had written that the police had sorted the Cobras out, and he'd not seen hardly anyone apart from a couple of fishermen with boats in the couple of months he'd lived there. The gang was probably long gone by now.

His phone pinged, making him jump. Hardly anyone knew his number.

He pulled it quickly from the charger to read the text.

'Thank you, Mr Cobain. I'm super-excited about coming to NZ. I look forward to finally meeting you.'

His stomach flipped. Mr Cobain. It sounded so formal. So excited to be coming out here. And so unsuspecting of who her boss really was.

The gnawing in his gut unsettled him. He never got like this, nervy and nauseous. It was real now. She would finally be with him again.

He put it down to the fear that she'd freak out and leave when she found out who exactly Mr Cobain was. He hated deceiving her. But he was only doing this to keep her safe.

He hoped she'd see it that way.

All he wanted, he told himself, was to have one chance to talk things through with her, tell her what really happened that night at the farmhouse. Anything more was too much to hope for.

CHAPTER 11

----------*----------

"I can't believe I've slept for fifteen hours straight!"

I'm embarrassed to find myself in my pyjamas in front of Celia. But she laughs it off as she strolls into the Lake Lodge kitchen.

I check the clock on the wall and cringe. It's three in the afternoon, for goodness sake!

Celia sets an apple pie she's baked for me onto the counter-top.

"Ah, thank you. That's so kind."

Smoothing my bed-head hair down, I go to fill the kettle.

"Sorry, about this. Guess my body's not set up for time travel."

"No worries, honey. That ole' jetlag's a bugger, I've heard."

"What a view!"

I almost drop the mug as I take in the lake.

I'd feasted on the lake view last night at dusk. You can't exactly miss it. And I'd done a quick nosy scoot around the lodge too, but I was so exhausted that within half an hour I'd crashed out, fast asleep.

But now, going through to the lounge area with our mugs of tea, I can see the full vista of the lake in the sunshine through those wonderful full-length shuttered windows.

"It's so beautiful here."

I'm already eyeing up the route along the shoreline where I'll go for a run later.

"And quiet. If you need anything, you give me a call, love. And you'll be coming over to our house for supper tomorrow, I hope?"

"You sure? I don't want to put you to any trouble."

"You're not. So I take that as a yes, then?"

"Yes! Thanks Celia."

My new neighbour smiles back at me.

We chat for a while, talking about Greece and my whistle-stop tour of Italy, and I get my camera out to show her.

"You take a pretty good photo. I love that one of the coloured houses on the cliffs."

"Cinque Terra. It was amazing. I went out on a boat to take those."

"You need to take some of the lake."

"Oh, I will. In the morning, when the light's best. Not that I've seen it yet."

I look down guiltily at my pyjamas.

"I've been dying to take Frank to Europe before we're too old," Celia says wistfully. "That shop of his, it's a millstone. Not been farther than Auckland in the last twenty years."

"Well, there are worse places to be."

"You're right, there."

She's gazing out at the lake too.

Now that we've broken the ice, I pluck up the courage to broach what I've been dying to ask.

"Uhh... my new employer, Mr Cobain," I throw in casually. "What's he like, then?"

"You not met him yet? Have you not had a skype call with him, or anything?"

Celia gives me a concerned mother look.

"*Struth!*"

"I answered an ad online a friend sent me. Then Mr Cobain texted me."

"So, how d'you know he's not an axe-murderer? Or that he's not one of them dodgy types that'll lock you up in a basement or'll sell you to a gang and auction you off for the Asian sex trade?"

"*Uhh ... I ...,*"

"Y' need to be more careful, love."

She shuts up abruptly, realising that I'm rattled.

And I am. I feel the knife on my neck again and the blood draining out of me as I go a little giddy.

"Honey, are you alright?"

She clucks over me, making me sit down on one of the green velvet sofas. She's staring at the scar on my neck.

"You've gone white as a ghost. My big mouth runs away with me sometimes. I've been watching too many films. You'll be fine here. Mr Cobain's a real gent."

"Yeah, he seems nice."

He'd left me a note on the worktop.

'Welcome to NZ'

It said that he'd stocked up the fridge and to make herself at home in any of the empty bedrooms.

"He said he'd call me once I've settled in."

I took the room at the front of the main house with a glorious view of the lake. It's next to the one his things are in. If that's awkward, I'll move.

"He's a Pom," Celia runs on, eager to recover things. "Early thirties, I'd say. But I think he might be…?"

Celia looks at me searchingly.

"What?"

"You know?" she adds conspiratorially, "I think…. he's… *batting for the other team*."

"You mean he's gay?"

"Frank says I'm a loony, but I've sussed him."

"Why d'ya think he's gay?"

"When I hinted about a couple of lovely girls who'd jump at meeting a handsome fulla like him, he says to me he's not interested."

"P'raps he's got a girlfriend?"

"And him out here, on his own? No, there's no one else, I'm sure of it. And y' gotta admit, he's pretty handy, eh? He's done this place up real tasteful. He's got that artistic eye *they have*, ya know, for colours and design and whatnot."

I relax a little and take a sip of tea.

"Hmm ... I did get the advert from this job sent to me by my gay friend."

I realise I'm adding more weight to Celia's theory.

"If Mr Cobain is anything like my friend Jason, I'll be fine."

Celia looks at me triumphantly.

"And he can't fish to save his life, sweetie," she shares with me in confidence. "So don't be thinking you'll be livin' on trout from the lake. The fish are quite safe from him. My advice to you, love, is to fill up your freezer."

After the morning madness of boys showering, getting their school stuff together and clamouring for their breakfasts, Shaun found daytime at the hostel eerily quiet. And if he was being honest, a little tedious.

In the mornings he helped with cleaning and laundry, shopped for groceries and prepared the boys' meals. In the afternoon he tried to go for a walk or he'd go with Ari to throw a line off the rocks into the sea.

What was it with Kiwis? Every time, Ari caught three, even four fish. He'd still caught nothing. Ari thought he might have better luck spear-fishing and promised to take him when the sea was calmer. He had a sniper's aim, after all. He hoped to God he'd be better at that.

Shaun checked his watch and felt that now familiar churn in his gut that came every time he thought about her. Claire had been at the lodge for two whole days.

When would be the appropriate time to contact her?

And if he called would she recognise his voice? Probably. It was too risky.

As her employer he needed to keep it formal. Dictate the terms of communication he concluded, overruling his impetuous fingers that were itching to video call her there and then.

Everyone was busy with homework and Ari was over at Michelle's parents' place, where he lived when he wasn't at the hostel. Mateo had his final exams coming up, so he'd hardly seen him and Rawiri had finished his work and was playing a video game. They were a good bunch of boys.

He sent her a short chat message. He hoped she'd settled into the lodge and that she was enjoying living at the lake. It was quite vanilla. But, it was all he could think to say.

There was no reply. Feeling restless, Shaun fetched Jake's diary from under the bed. He needed something to distract his thoughts.

January 17th

The weather's been real hot lately. I think we might be in for a drought. The lake level's dropped to the lowest I seen since I've been here and I'm visiting all the campers reminding them about the fire ban. Nine times out of ten they're as good as gold.

Every day over the last few days I seen them Cobras buzzing around on bikes near the lake. Something's off. Never had no bother in ten years from them, and all of a sudden it's like they're circling.

I called the station about it. Mikey says that they'll keep an eye. They'll probably send a squad car this way when they're up north next.

Perhaps it's just me, but I kind of feel protective of these two. They've been with me a week now, and even though I shouldn't get attached, that little one she's as cute as. A bright little button of a thing she is.

Her mum got a bit munted last night on the wine and let it all slip out. First time she's said anything about why they're here. The little girl's dad was mixed up in drugs in London. An accountant or something like that, she said. Anyways she was the main witness at the trial.

It explains why it's taken a good week to get rid of that strung out look of hers, but she's starting to relax a bit more now. Get used to our Kiwi ways.

Shaun's head was spinning. He'd presumed the place was a

weekend fishing retreat. But it was, in fact, a safe house all along. He flicked through the diary, there was one entry left and it was short.

Jan 24th

All I can think is that they've had a tip-off from someone. How else would they've known?

Why else would they have tried to shoot Chantelle and little Isla?

I put the fire in the kitchen out before it could take hold. It was damn lucky I heard the glass smash or those petrol bombs would of done for the whole place. Bastards would've torched us in our beds.

The police whisked the two away right there and then. In the middle of the night.

I called my man in the consulate the next day but he was clammed up tighter than a gnat's arse too. Would only tell me that they're both safe. That's good I suppose. But I miss them and I don't mind saying it. It was nice having them around.

It's real quiet here now, though there's plenty for me to do. The pot-shots those Cobras took went right through the roof on the west side wing and it'll need fixing before the winter rains set in. I've boarded up the kitchen as best I can 'til I get some glass.

A shiver ran through him as he began to join the dots. He flicked through the diary. There were no more entries. He couldn't leave it like this, he needed to know more.

Did the Cobras have a contract to kill the woman and the girl?

Posing as a hitman he knew how the contracts worked. Like some old-fashioned wanted poster in a Wild West saloon bar. Wanted Dead or Alive. Only now it was posted up on the dark web. And somewhere, on an encrypted message board in cyberspace was a wanted poster, a contract out on him too.

He only had half the tale. What had happened afterwards to Jake?

He grabbed his phone.

"Frank, it's Shaun."

He hoped he didn't sound rude but this couldn't wait. He had Claire out at the lake. He needed to check that the threat was gone.

The line was a little crackly with a poor signal.

"I've read Jake's diary. I need to know. Was he killed by the Cobras?"

He talked softly into his phone in his room, hoping that his voice wouldn't carry and the boys couldn't hear him.

Frank confirmed the worst.

He told him everything. It was a relief, Frank admitted. He hadn't known what to do for the best. Keep it zipped or blab.

According to Frank, the bikers had returned two nights after. And they were royally pissed off for missing their bounty. Frank said the newspaper reported that they'd tied Jake up. Frank reckoned they'd tried to get Jake to spill where the woman and her little girl had been moved to. Of course, he didn't have a clue. So they shot him dead, afraid Jake would rat them out to the police.

Shaun's mind was racing.

His instincts had been right. Those holes he'd seen sprayed into the living room walls, they were bullet holes. No wonder the Brits wanted to dispose of the place. Once the Cobras had rumbled the safe house, it was unusable after.

So, why had they given it to him? Was it no longer a risk now that things had calmed down, or had they simply thought that with his background that he could handle the Cobras?

Frank promised over the phone to keep a close eye on Claire, though they both convinced themselves by the end of the call that things were a lot different now and that Jake's shooting had been a one-off, thank God. Still, Frank didn't know about the contract that was out on Shaun. And he didn't know that Claire had been tracked down halfway across Europe.

Shaun tried to think about it rationally. The Scousers were hardly the Mafia. And anyway, it was a bloody long way from New Brighton to New Zealand.

It was late in the evening when Claire responded to him.

Claire: Mr Cobain? Is that you?

His heart pounded when he saw the reply notification flash up on his screen.

Shaun: Call me Shaun, please. Have you recovered from your flight?
Claire: Yes. Though I'm still waking up wanting to eat in the middle of the night. Your place is amazing. It's so tranquil here.

That was a relief. She liked the place. He thought about his response. What if he confessed to her right there and then? Admit to her who he was. How would she react?

No, he chickened out, he needed to keep in role for now. Until he was more sure about things.

Shaun: You ready for some work?
Claire: Yes. Of course. I noticed the bedrooms in one wing need repainting. Do you want me to start on those?
Shaun: Good idea
Claire: Any particular colour?
Shaun: You decide
Claire: You sure? Celia and I were complimenting your interior design skills. You've got a great eye for colours, so I'm super-nervous about getting it wrong

Shaun was puzzled. Most of the paint he'd used were neutrals and greys.

Shaun: You won't. The pots I've used are in the barn. Use the same colours, if you're not sure
Claire: I'm so grateful to my friend for sending me the advert for this job. Do you know Jason?

Dammit! Had she sussed him out?

Shaun: Jason?
Claire: Oh. Never mind. It was a long shot. He said that the advert

was from a friend
Shaun: That's possible, I sent it to lots of people
Claire: Jason's an airline pilot. Says he'd like to come over sometime to visit if that'd be alright?

This was getting complicated.

Shaun: Sure. Once the bedrooms are painted, there'll be plenty of space for guests
Claire: Great. He's gay. And single
Shaun: You trying to hook me up?
Claire: No!

The typing paused. She was obviously embarrassed. What was going on in her head? Did she think that he was gay too? Where had that come from?

Celia. He bet she'd jumped to conclusions after he'd closed down her attempts at matchmaking.

Amused, he stretched back onto his single bed. Never mind, her assumptions might help ease things between them.

Shaun: Good night, Claire
Claire: Good night, Shaun. Thanks again for the opportunity

CHAPTER 12

--------*--------

"Want summat to eat?"

Irish signalled over towards the prison officer for permission to move.

"Yeah, okay," Tony agreed.

The guard gave them the nod.

Tony wedged the second magazine that his brother had got through security into the elasticated waistband of his joggers.

Together they made their way over to the hatch at the far end of the hall. Visitors could buy a cup of tea or a bite to eat there. And the time-served lags who manned it were doing 'through the gate' training for a national sandwich chain, their promised employment on release.

"How's Mum?"

Tony's eyes scanned around shiftily as they queued up at the hatch.

Irish sensed his unease. Even here, in full view of the guards, you had to watch your back. Especially now he was carrying thousands of pounds worth of psychoactive infused paper rolled up in his joggers.

"Fine. She misses you. Says she'll come up in a fortnight and bring baby Leighton with her."

"Ah, that'll be nice. I can't wait to see him again. Hope he'll know I'm his dad."

Irish sniffed.

"Don't be daft. 'Course he will."

It was the baby's mother Tony needed to worry about. From the Snapchat pictures of her out clubbing, she didn't look like she was missing Tony much these days.

He'd sent her a little warning though. The pinkie of the lad she'd copped off with in the club. It would be a memorable shag for that bloke.

"I'm starving. Wanna soup?"

"Yeah. Okay."

He fixed his eyes on the balding man behind the counter.

"Whitey? How you doin' la?"

The older man nodded back.

"Not bad, Irish. A bit of luck, and I'll be out soon."

He took in the logo on Whitey's apron; 'Sandwich Artist in Training.'

"You gonna be spreadin' butties when ya get out then, eh?

"Summat like that."

"Great career choice, Whitey. Plenty of dough in that, I hear."

"Yeah, I see what ya did there. Very fuckin' funny."

The portly female officer by his shoulder coughed.

Irish nodded towards the large urn on the counter.

"What's the soup?"

"It's fuckin' chicken."

The officer cleared her throat loudly.

"John, we talked about this," she reprimanded him. "You can't talk to customers like that. It's not *fucking* chicken is it?"

Whitey opened the lid and carefully studied the contents of the steaming pot.

"Sorry, Miss. No, you're dead right. It's not *fuckin'* chicken."

He gave Irish and his kid brother a cheeky wink.

"It's fuckin' *tomato*."

Irish snorted.

"Two *fuckin'* tomato soups it is then, Whitey."

The officer humphed, and the men sniggered their way back to their table.

"Little victories," he reflected out loud, sitting back down with his brother. "It's the only way to survive this place. Don't let the bastards get to yer, our kid."

They sipped at the tepid soup for a minute or so.

Irish studied Tony's face distorting into a frown. The way it always did when he was wrangling with something.

"What's up?"

"Why d'ya call him Whitey? We all know his name's John Cullen. He lives 'round the corner from our Nan."

Irish stared at his little brother. Was he always this stupid?

"'Cos he drives the van. Does the deliveries."

"Yeah, but… his van, it's not even white?"

"It was once, alright."

A sulky silence settled between them.

He looked back towards his brother. Tony wasn't letting this go, he could tell.

"But… he had a black one. I know, 'cos when I was a kid I robbed it."

"Shut up will yer."

Irish's voice became a gruff whisper.

"We can't go changin' his name every single time he changes the colour of his soddin' van, can we? That'd be stupid. He's Whitey, okay! End of."

"Jesus, don't do yer nut in. I was only askin'."

"Look, I'm sorry, alright? Whitey owes me a favour or two. He'll look after you in here."

Irish met his brother's eye.

"Sandwich artist, my arse."

"Yeah," Tony smirked back, "He'll never live that one down."

You need anything, our kid, if there's any bother, you get word to Whitey, alright?"

Tony nodded.

"I will. Don't you worry nutin' about me."

He was glad to hear that others from the firm were here somewhere. It made things easier, having associates in there, even if they were on other wings. And being Irish's brother counted for a lot.

"You managed to track down the grass yet?" Tony asked him under his breath.

His eye twitched. He'd lost count of the dead ends and false sightings he'd fielded in the last few weeks. And now, since Mac had botched things up, Edwards' bird had gone cold too. No postings. No nothing.

"Let it go, bruv."

"Can't."

"Why?"

"'Leave it, Tone. I can't, alright?

His little brother was doing it again. Needling him. He always could call him out. Spot his weaknesses.

"He's harmed my family so he's a dead man walking."

Tony shrugged.

"Okay Don Connoroni, I believe ya. And it's not at all 'cos he shafted you."

Connor caught his brother's eye and fired him a warning shot.

Tony slumped sulkily back in his seat making him feel even worse. It wasn't easy doing time.

His little brother had aged a fair bit since he'd seen him last. His face now had that familiar grey pallor to it. Prison did that to you. The monotonous routine, the stodgy food and the long hours stuck in your cell.

"I can't leave it. Okay? Not while you're banged up in here."

"Then find her, if it'll make you happy," Tony suggested. "With that scar, she should be easy enough to spot. Put a contract out on her too."

"I can't believe that I'm here. Every morning I wake up and I drink a mug of coffee sitting on the porch step looking out at the lake."

I'm talking online to Annie who's sitting in The Cross Keys pub with Jac. It's evening there, of course. And it looks like they've lit the fires in the pub. Cosy. I'm out of whack here. I've forgotten that it's autumn back in Wales.

It's so good to see them both, I haven't spoken with them since Greece. And seeing them here in front of me, in the pub, is making me feel more than a little homesick.

Jac's face appears on the screen.

"What's it like there?"

"Look I'll show you."

I get up and pan the camera of my phone around to show them the lake and then the lodge behind me.

"That's so gorgeous," I hear Annie exclaim. "You lucky thing."

"And you're there, all on your own?"

I can hear a hint of concern in Jac's voice.

I roll my eyes at the screen.

"I'm fine. It's peaceful here. I'm enjoying having some space to think about stuff. It's like being on the top of a mountain at home. Only here, it's by a lake."

"What jobs are you expected to do?"

"There's not exactly a list. But painting and cleaning, mostly. Oh! And I've mended the chicken coop."

"You got hens?"

Jac perks up. He can talk for hours about farming.

"No. Only a feral rooster so far. Frank, my neighbour, says his name's Rowdy. I've been putting feed out but he's sneaky, he raids the food and flies away."

"He needs some ladies. Get him some hens," Jac chips in.

Annie pulls a face.

"Do you get lonely?"

"I've been jogging around the shoreline every afternoon and I've got a pickup truck so I can get to town. And tomorrow, I'm going to a barbecue at a neighbour's place."

"Good, you're getting to know the locals."

"Yeah, they've been great. But the invite's a bit odd. On the text, it says to bring a plate? I'd've thought they wanted some wine or beer?"

"Perhaps they don't drink?" Annie suggests. "And what's this boss of yours like?"

"He's away for a few weeks, working in a hostel up north. But he messages me at night to check how I'm doing. He's a nice guy."

"And?..."

I can see that Annie's fishing. I grin back at her.

"What?"

"You like him. I can tell," she says, shifting position and grabbing her orange juice.

"He's totally gay."

I smack that one down straight away. It's typical of my luck because Shaun Cobain is really nice and I hate to admit that I've got a little crush on him brewing.

"And... uh, we've got some news for you too."

Annie shifts the camera onto the both of them and I can see her grabbing hold of Jac's hand.

"What?"

"We're not gonna be able to come out and see you for a bit, I'm afraid."

They've got a farm so I wasn't exactly expecting them to visit any time soon.

"What she means," Jac chips in, "Is that we're expecting a baby."

"Oh, wow!" I squeal. "I so wish I was there to give you a huge hug! Congratulations!"

"Yes," Annie beams, "It's been a bit of a shock. And really bad planning, 'cos he or she's making an appearance in April, right in the middle of lambing."

It's lovely news but the call leaves me feeling flat.

Annie and Jac are moving forward with their lives and from the call I can tell that they're happy together.

But what about me? What am I doing? And who would want me with this scar?

I shake myself and refuse to waste any more time feeling sorry for myself. I've done enough of that.

But still, I decide, if I was to settle down it would be somewhere like here.

The Bootle boozer was lively, even on a Tuesday afternoon. And most of the drinkers recognised Irish as he walked past them with his friends towards the bar.

"Whitey, what'll you be havin'?"

"Err, Guinness, Irish. That's very kind of you."

"Two pints of the black stuff and two triple Jamieson chasers please, love."

"Gerrit down ya!"

Three mates alongside Irish slapped Whitey's back as he downed his first full pint of Guinness in two gulps.

"And how does that taste?"

"Like freedom."

He laughed and toasted him with the whisky.

"Sláinte!"

"Sláinte!" they echoed back and emptied their glasses only to have them refilled again.

"So… about this sandwich job ya got?" Irish ribbed.

Whitey smirked.

"Yeah, what about that. Giz us a week and I'll be coughin' and pickin' me arse outta that one, don't you worry, la'"

Irish slapped his back.

"Good to have yer back on the firm. And how's our kid doin'?"

"Tony's alright. Don't you be worrying about yer brother, he's onto a good number with that magic paper of his. As long as he keeps getting hold of them bike magazines."

"Don't you worry about that. I've signed him up for a monthly subscription," Irish joked, feeling into his pocket as his phone vibrated.

Whitey watched as Irish's face transformed.

"What d'ya mean, he didn't deliver?" he growled into the phone.

He looked across at Whitey, his phone on mute.

"Fancy doin' us a job this week? A thievin' scally over in Toxteth needs a new pair of boots."

"Concrete ones, Irish?"

He sniffed in agreement.

"And a good dunk head-first into the Mersey. That's *after* he tells me where my five grand is. I'm not wasting my time on this one. You chop him till he squeals."

Whitey swallowed his second pint down as Irish ended the call.

There was a notification on the fake Facebook site he'd created. He clicked onto it.

It said that his Facebook friend, Claire Williams, had been tagged into a picture.

"What the fu…"

The picture was of a woman's slightly rounded stomach with the message underneath,

'Great to see Claire Williams on FB today. Now even New Zealand has heard our news. Can't wait until March!'

"Lads, I've gotta go."

"*Argh! Eh?* Come on, Irish. Whatever it is'll wait."

"Sorry boys."

He nodded to the girl and stuck a hundred quid behind the bar for them. Then he reached into his pocket and pulled out a set of keys, pressing them into Whitey's hands.

"What's this?"

"Yer new van. For collections and deliveries."

"Thanks, Irish."

"It's white. And don't you be changing the feckin' colour again."

Whitey laughed appreciatively.

"I'll give yer a call when I've done the job."

He clenched Whitey's shoulder.

"Get me back my five grand, alright?"

"No problem, Irish."

Feeling the chill of the autumn air as he came out of the dark boozer into the afternoon light, Irish reread the Facebook notification.

It could be nothing. Claire Williams was backpacking around

the world, but at least now he had a lead.

The contract would be easy enough to put out to New Zealand. He didn't know much about the outfits there, but he was sure there'd be some badass boys who'd like to earn a few quid.

And as for Claire Williams, she was collateral damage. As his dear old dad had taught him, to catch a big fish you need to use live bait.

Every night for the week she'd been living at the lake, once the boys were settled in their rooms for the night Shaun had been messaging Claire.

Claire: Hi Shaun, are you free to chat?

He couldn't help but smirk when he saw the message come in. It was the best part of his day, speaking with her.

Shaun: Hey! What've you been up to?
Claire: I went for a swim last night.
Shaun: You did?

A picture of Claire swimming in the lake invaded his mind and flooded his senses.

Claire: Yeah. Good job no one was about 'cos the moon was out and it made me do something a bit mad. I got up and walked down to stand on the shore and then, I don't know why, but I slipped into the water. Did you ever do that?

This was too much.

Shaun: No
Claire: Oh God, I'm sorry I told you that. It was weird, wasn't it?
Shaun: Did it feel weird to you at the time?
Claire: Yes.
Shaun: So, what made you do it?
Claire: No idea. It was a spur-of-the-moment kinda thing. I thought,

'what the hell?' It's so not like me.

Shaun: And was it cold?

Claire: No, it was so warm. And the sky was so clear. I floated on my back and looked up. I swear, it was like the stars were dripping out of the sky.

Shaun: The southern stars are so much brighter

Claire: Yeah. I've never seen so many and so big.

Shaun: Sounds like a magical moment.

Claire: It was.

That pang again as he thought about the stars, about her. God! How he wished he'd been there too. With her.

He cleared his throat, trying to squash his image of Claire with the pearl light on her olive skin and her sleek dark hair, floating naked on the top of the quick-silvered water.

He tried to focus, changing the subject.

Shaun: You've been here a week now. How are you enjoying it?

Claire: I love it.

Shaun: Not too quiet?

Claire: A little. I went around to Frank and Celia's for a barbecue last night and I'm getting to know a few people in the town.

Shaun: That's good.

Claire: It was a bit embarrassing, actually. Did you know that 'bring a plate' means to bring some food?

Shaun: Ah!

Claire: Yep... I did apologise. I thought they didn't like washing up or something. But they were laughing so hard, that it was all okay

He could imagine Celia's reaction. She was sure to be telling everyone about that faux pas for the next week.

But she had admitted too that she was a little lonely. Was it too isolated for her out at the lake? Was it boring her? How could he keep her occupied? Keep her there?

Shaun: What do you want from this job, Claire?

Claire: The challenge of getting stuck into something new, doing the best job I can.

Shaun: It's not an interview question. I'm curious, that's all. Come on, Claire, what is it you're trying to get from coming out here?

There was a break in typing.

Claire: I need a bit of time out. I want to figure out what I want to do next.
Shaun: What are you running away from, Claire?
Claire: Myself. I need to stop running and find myself.
Shaun: Is that because you feel lost?

Another pause.

Claire: To be honest I'm a little tired, do you mind if we talk tomorrow?
Shaun: That's fine. Goodnight, Claire

He rubbed his face.
She'd signed off, closed the conversation down. He'd pushed her too far.

CHAPTER 13

--------- ✶ ---------

The tears roll down my face as I see what Annie's posted. She's tagged me in her photo. She's only gone and told the whole world where I am. Of course, she wasn't to know.

I messaged her as soon as I saw it on Facebook and she took it down immediately. But it's been there for a couple of days, and the Scousers have inevitably seen that I'm here in New Zealand.

Nowhere feels safe anymore. Will I ever be free from them?

I've messaged Jason too.

He insists I tell Shaun immediately.

That means coming clean about everything. Telling him about the Scousers. What if he thinks I'm too high risk? And that I'll bring trouble to his door? What if he tells me to go?

Weighing it up, I haven't got much choice.

Wiping my face dry, I start to type.

Claire: Shaun, are you there?

It's a good five minutes before the phone pings. Five minutes of pacing up and down the porch, trying to get my words and my shit together.

Shaun: Hi Claire. Are you alright?

It's the middle of the day, and I bet he's figuring that it's odd for me to be messaging him.

Claire: The other night you asked if I was running away from some-
thing?
Shaun: And are you?
Claire: I'm scared in case you ask me to leave
Shaun: I'd never do that, Claire. I promise. What is it? Please tell me.

He sounds so concerned. It's weird but I feel uncannily close to
him; connected somehow.

Claire: You were right the other night. I am running
Shaun: What's happened?
Claire: I'm running away from something bad that happened to me
Shaun: Are you in danger?
Claire: No. Nothing like that. I was involved with someone. It's a long
story
Shaun: Tell me
Claire: The guy was an informant and some bad people found out. I
got attacked by them
Shaun: Did they hurt you?
Claire: Yeah. I have a scar. Down my neck. It's horrible. And now I'm
hideous, Shaun

There, I've said it.

Shaun: Show me
Claire: No
Shaun: Send me a picture. I want to see your face

Shaking, I hold up the phone and press the button. I can hardly
bear to look at the image I'm sending him.

Shaun: You're beautiful, Claire
Claire: Please don't
Shaun: But you are

Hollow words. He's trying to make me feel better and that
makes it so much worse.

Shaun: You're upset. Why are you telling me this now?

Claire: A criminal gang called the Scousers, they're after the person I was with. He disappeared and they've been following me, thinking I'll lead them to him, which is ridiculous. First, they tracked me to Greece, and now they've found out I'm here
Shaun: How?
Claire: My friend Annie posted it on Facebook. She's deleted it but it's probably too late

He's a long time silent. I'm positive he's regretting his promise not to get rid of me.

Shaun: Bloody Facebook! Do they know where in New Zealand?
Claire: No
Shaun: I wouldn't worry, then. It's a big country with two islands and where we are is pretty far from everyone. You'll be safe. They won't find you here
Claire: You think?
Shaun: Trust me
Claire: Okay
Shaun: If you see anyone acting strange, call the police and call me. I'll come straight over. And if you're worried, I can call Frank and Celia, and see if you can stay at theirs
Claire: No please, don't do that. I'll be fine. You're right, this country's massive and remote, and I haven't seen anyone for days
Shaun: You sure you'll be alright on your own? I can give up the job and come back?
Claire: No! You can't do that. Ari needs you
Shaun: Hmm
Claire: I'll be okay. Honestly. If there's anything suspicious, I'll call the police
Shaun: Good
Shaun: Did you love him?

The question surprises me but now's not the time for lies.

Claire: Yes, I did. But, I did a terrible thing to him
Shaun: What?

Claire: I presumed that he was one of the bad guys too. And I can never tell him how wrong I was. Shaun, you don't want to listen to this, you've been a big help, putting things into perspective when I was losing it
Shaun: Why can't you ever tell him you're sorry, Claire?

He pushes it, and although I don't want to go into it I feel obligated.

Claire: 'Cos it's too late.
Shaun: Why's it too late?
Claire: 'Cos it's complicated. And I'm never going to see him again and there's no way to contact him, so that's that.
Shaun: What? Is he on the space station or something?
Claire: No.
Shaun: Dead?
Claire: No. Just gone. Actually, you remind me so much of him. The way we talk.

There's no response. Great! I tell him a drug gang is hunting me down. He's cool with that. I blurt out that Sion reminds me of him and he loses the plot.
Then it dawns on me. The scar. What did I expect?
Another message comes in.

Shaun: So, what are you going to do next?
Claire: Use this time to pick myself up, start again
Shaun: Sounds like a good idea

Wanting to move to safer ground, I decide to share my plans to search for my Dad.

Claire: Yeah. I'd like to find my father. He's from New Zealand. That's why I took this job. I wanted to come here to find him. Tane Matene is the name on my birth certificate. Don't know anything else, though.
Shaun: I'll help you if you like?
Claire: You will? I'd appreciate that

It's so strange, telling him everything has made me feel so

much safer. I need to squash that crush. He's gay anyway. But, I do want to keep him as a friend.

Claire Thanks for listening, Shaun
Shaun: Anytime
Claire: Do you find this strange?
Shaun: What?
Claire: This. The way we talk together. It's like I've known you forever
Shaun: Yes, I feel it too, Claire. It's good, it means that we'll work together well
Claire: Yeah
Shaun: Anything at all, you call me alright? And Claire?
Claire: Yes?
Shaun: I know you've already dismissed my words. But you need to believe me. You're still beautiful

I wipe my face and take a deep breath. He's made me feel so much better. And totally depressed. Because no matter how hard I try to talk myself out of it, I'm fast developing a huge and annoyingly futile crush on this gay man.

"Did ya see me go up that rock, Shaun? It was as sweet as."
Rawiri thumped the back of his seat and Ari took his hand off the minibus steering wheel to nudge him
"Shaun?"
"Oh, sorry. Did ya say something?"
"Rawiri was talkin' to himself for a good ten minutes back there, mate."
Rawiri, who was leaning forward in the seat behind Shaun, sniggered as Ari raised an eyebrow ironically in the rearview mirror.
Shaun turned around.
"Sorry, pal."
They'd been out into the forest with the boys doing their first

climbing lesson. Shaun had managed to borrow some climbing gear from an outdoor centre over on the east coast and he'd been teaching them basic moves, knots and clippings.

In the army, he'd gained instructor qualifications in quite a few outdoor pursuits as part of his transition back to civilian life. He couldn't use the certificates now, but he remembered what to do.

They'd even begun to have a little climb up the volcanic rock that Ari had found for them. It had been perfect for beginners with its rough, grippy surface. Already the boys were asking to go again, and they were only in the minibus on the way home.

"You gonna tell me what's up or am I gonna have to guess?" Ari said quietly to Shaun.

Rawiri, earwigging, egged him on from behind.

"Go on Ari. Have a guess."

"Nah, it'd make him blush."

Ari let out a big, hearty laugh and Shaun shook his head.

"It's nothing. I've got a few things on my mind, that's all. About the place I'm renovating."

"Yeah, whatever," Rawiri sniggered to Ari. "Bet it's a chick, eh?"

"Hey!"

Ari caught Rawiri's eye in the rearview mirror.

"I can pull his leg, but when you do it, you cross the line."

"No need to rark up! I was only sayin'."

From the mirror Shaun could see Rawiri momentarily slumping backwards in a huff, then turning to chat with the other boys.

"Ari?" Shaun ventured.

"Yeah."

"There's this girl I know."

"You managed to snag yourself a bird, bro?"

"Yeah, no, I mean, she's a mate of mine. British. She's trying to track her dad. How would she go about it over here?"

"Council office in Daragrei's a good start, take a look through the electoral roll? Does she know where he is? North or South Island?"

"Nah - she only has a name. Tane Matene."

"Spell the first name?"

"T-A-N-E"

"Shit! That's…"

Rawiri was listening in again. Ari's eye caught his eye in the rearview mirror, and Rawiri promptly turned back to speak with the boys.

"That's a common name."

"So, no-one you know of?"

"Yeah… Nah, bro…" Ari brushed it off casually, thinking aloud, "And I wouldn't waste their time searching for him up North. I think the Matene surname's from the South Island somewhere. Or perhaps out Gisborne way, eh?"

"Ah, alright. I'll let her know. I told her it wouldn't be easy."

Shaun looked at the view out of the window as the fern-edged road tracked the estuary back towards the sea and the hostel.

He'd been dying to put a kayak in the water. He needed to buy one once he was done at the hostel. The estuary looked ideal for a paddle.

"Ari, when are you planning on testing out the waka?"

"Next weekend. Hope you're gonna help us out. Need your muscles, bro."

"Why?"

Rawiri piped up.

"'Cos, it's bloody heavy."

"Glad I'm useful for something."

Shaun turned and gave Rawiri a big grin.

Rawiri reminded him of what he'd been like as a kid. Full-on, desperately wanting someone to pay him a little bit of attention, give him a bit of time.

His phone pinged. He'd asked Claire to send him pictures every day. He could tell from their messaging that she'd lost a huge amount of confidence because of her scar. She wasn't the same bubbly bartender he'd known back in The Cross Keys.

He felt bad about that every time they talked. If only he'd have been able to stop her from getting hurt that day. But he'd been too far away. And what was done was done. All he could do now was help her to feel good about herself again.

The first pictures he'd asked for were of her work. The newly painted rooms.

Then he'd asked for one with her in it. She'd been reluctant at first, but eventually a selfie pinged through, paintbrush in hand.

And then another. Her beside the chicken coop she'd rebuilt. Done a good job too.

Then, a surprise. She sent one of herself posing with a bag of seed potatoes by a veggie patch she'd dug out.

Small steps, but even if she didn't realise it she was gaining in confidence every day.

His pulse raced as he scrolled again through all the pictures she'd sent him. She really was beautiful and he couldn't wait until he saw her again.

I've taken to sitting on the wooden porch looking out at the lake as the sun drops, messaging Shaun. In a few short weeks, he's become my bestie.

A photo comes through and I laugh out loud. I told him, fair's fair. He needed to send me pics too.

So far I've had shots of the sea, the hostel and a beautifully carved canoe.

And each time there's a bit of Shaun in it.

Mystery man. He's teased me. Given me an arm, a leg, a shoulder. And now this. His silhouette. The back of a man, arms and legs spread out as he climbs up a rock.

I open it and try to zoom in. His head's covered by a plastic helmet and I've only got the back of him to go on. But it's enough to make my heart thump. He's tan and tall. Wearing shorts and a t-shirt. Well defined muscular shoulders, tight arse and strong athletic legs. He's a regular action man. Typical of my luck that he prefers men.

Claire: I can see what you've been doing today

Shaun: Hi Claire, not long got back from the forest. I'd forgotten how much I love rock climbing
Claire: Sounds fun. I'd love to have a try
Shaun: I'll take you

My heart is pumping fast now. Is that a date?

Claire: Will you?
Shaun: Definitely. What've you been up to?
Claire: Finished painting the last bedroom. Feeling very proud of myself, I don't mind telling you
Shaun: You're my employee of the month. Well done
Claire: Hmm. Out of how many?... Scrub that. I already know
Shaun: So, that's the last of them?
Claire: Yip. And to celebrate I had a long, hot soak in the tub afterwards. How I've managed to get paint flecks onto some places of my anatomy is a complete mystery

There I go again. I know I shouldn't. But there's something about him, I can't help it. He makes me want to flirt.

Shaun: Naked painting, was it?

And laugh. Is *he* flirting with me, now? I've been wondering that for a while. Jason's never like this.

Claire: Good job I wasn't naked. Vern from the hardware store came out to the lake with some chooks for me this afternoon. I nearly fell off the ladder when I heard him calling out
Shaun: I now have hens?
Claire: Yeah. About that
Shaun: It's fine, Claire. I was going to get some myself
Claire: You were? Phew. I couldn't get Rowdy in the coop and he looked so lonely up in the tree. Then, Vern called me about some new layers of his
Shaun: How many did you get?
Claire: Six. And Rowdy's down from the tree already, hanging out with his girls. Hopefully, it won't be too long before there are eggs

Shaun: I'll look forward to that when I'm home. I'm looking forward
to seeing you too
  Claire: You are?
  Shaun: Yes
  Claire: Me too

What is he doing to me? I'm trembling.

Shaun: Has there been anyone strange or suspicious around?
Claire: No. Only Vern :)
Shaun: Good. Sleep tight, Claire
Claire: Goodnight, Shaun

CHAPTER 14

--------*--------

'*Kia Ora from New Zealand,*

One of my boys seen the dark-haired girl with a scar down her neck that you're looking for. She's staying out by us. I need five thousand pounds wired to the account below.

Once we get that we can talk.

Cobra King'

Irish read the message in his encrypted mail again. It was the right country. He hadn't said anything about location on the contract he'd put out globally on Claire Williams. But five thousand quid? That was bloody steep without supplying any proof. And this 'Cobra King'? Who the Hell was he?

'*I'll wire you a thousand. The other four you get once you send me photographs of her.*

Irish'

Sitting at his desk, he played with the paperclip in his hand, stretching the bends out until it was a straight piece of wire again. Bending it hard in two, the wire snapped in his fingers.

Was he any closer?

Perhaps. There was still not a sniff on Sion Edwards. But this was a waiting game and he'd have to be patient a little while longer.

Painting the rooms with the same colours as the pots in the shed, no problem.

But, now Shaun says he wants me to order the furnishings and I have a budget and a card to pay for it all.

This should be every woman's dream job. Isn't it supposed to be in our DNA? But, honestly, I haven't got a clue what I'm doing.

I'm so terrified about getting it wrong that I flip out on the phone to Celia. She tells me to get my butt over to the café in town tout-suite.

The eatery is an incongruously uber-artsy joint in this rural outpost of a town. I order a flat white and search for Celia who I find with her friend in the back courtyard.

"Claire, this is Tia."

Celia introduces me to a stylish young woman with long wavy brown hair. Straightaway the wonderful piece of carved jade she's wearing around her neck tells me that she's artsy. As opposed to me, I think a little self-consciously in my plain black t-shirt and paint-flecked cargo pants.

"Kia Ora, Claire."

She greets me with a pristine smile.

"Tia owns this place."

The back of the cafe is a walled garden, stuffed with tropical plants in pots and covered overhead in strings of garlanding light bulbs.

"Bought it on a whim. Been the bane of my life and the joy of it ever since."

"It's very cool."

Like her.

Celia presses on.

"Tia trained as a designer. She can help you."

"Thank God!"

She's surprised by the strong hug I give her.

"I'm way out of my depth."

Tia gets out her phone and shows me pictures of bedrooms.

"Keep it plain. Buy neutral colours for the bedding."

Celia sips her coffee.

"Especially if it's for paying guests. You'll be needing to keep them freshly updated."

I hadn't thought of that. I'm like a sponge soaking up their every word.

I see what she means. The art and the cushions pop out the colour but everything else is muted.

She promises to come up to the lake lodge later in the afternoon to help to get me going. I'm so thankful, she has no idea. Celia is a miracle-worker.

As soon as I'm back at the lodge, I disappear down the Google rabbit hole, scouring the internet for bedroom ideas and looking at the colours so that I can have some ideas to show Tia.

It's more fun than I thought, and I get carried away. So much so, that when I hear the sound of her SUV pulling up outside the lodge, I realise that the groceries I bought in town are still lying in their bags on the countertop.

"Hey! Come on in, I'm a woman obsessed!"

"I always wanted to see inside this place."

Tia glides into the kitchen. She's effortlessly cool, I think enviously as she floats around the place like an exotic butterfly, while I'm shoving things into the fridge.

"Ahh, the living room."

"Yeah, I love the windows and the view."

"Whose idea was it to paint over the wood on the walls with white?"

"Shaun's. He's the owner."

"I love it. It feels kinda Scandi."

"That's the problem. He's great at this, which makes it ten times worse if I stuff it up."

She tuts and brushes that idea away with her hand.

"Gimme a tiki tour of the rooms."

We spend all afternoon measuring and evaluating each room.

The space, the light, the colour. I'm learning so much. Then I grab the laptop so we can go online to find ideas and stockists.

She stares at my photo on the screen background. It's one I took of the lake. It was early morning and there was a mist rolling across it. It's one of my favourites.

"Who did that?"

I grin at her and shrug.

"You got some more?"

Standing on the porch I hug her again. This time it's with genuine affection, not like this morning when I clung to her like a life raft in the ocean.

I've hammered Shaun's credit card pretty hard but it's still way below the budget he gave me.

She won't hear of me paying for her time.

"Ten percent commission on those pictures is good enough for me."

We've ordered a set of canvases from my lake photos for her café. I'm really not sure that she'll be able to sell them all but I don't want to dampen her enthusiasm.

Tia smiles at me.

"This was fun. Monday night at the café, we've got a girl's night goin' on. Please say you'll come?"

"I'd love to."

Today has been one of the best here. I hadn't realised how lonely I'd become out at the lake.

"Who's that?"

She sweeps her long, dark hair over her shoulder and looks over to the shoreline to where a huge bald man with a long beard is taking photographs of the lake. "You seen him before?"

"No. I've not seen anyone really, the odd fisherman and family come up for the day. That's it."

My attention is drawn to the telephoto lens.

"He's got a professional bit of kit there. He's probably a twitcher."

"A what?"

"A birdwatcher."

"But the guy was taking snaps of the lodge and us on the deck."

"The place does look so pretty by the shore, don't you think? He looks like he's a professional photographer."

Tia stares at him doubtfully. The back of his leather jacket has a large snake on it.

"Not sure about that. And no way will his snaps be as good as yours. I'll stay here 'til here's gone."

She's being overly cautious. I guess it's because he's a big guy and he looks a little intimidating. But he can't help that. Working behind a bar has taught me that some of the toughest looking biker blokes are the biggest softies at heart.

He wanders peacefully away along the beach and a few minutes later we hear the unmistakable popping of his Harley Davidson telling us he's moved off.

"It's a bit lonely out here, Claire."

Tia looks concerned.

"When did ya say your boss is back?"

"Another couple of weeks."

"If you want to take a break and come crash out at the beach with me, just say. Any time. I mean it. I've plenty of space. And if you have any agro out here, you give me a call. I'll get my brothers out to you right away."

"Thanks. Honest, Tia, I'll be fine. But I'll see ya Monday night, yeah?"

Shaun's heart leapt when he heard the familiar sound of an incoming message. Claire was online. He grabbed the phone from the charger and lay back on his small hostel bed to read what she'd sent him. He laughed out loud. It was a warning. She'd been spending his money.

Claire: Don't have a blue fit when you see your bank account, okay? I'm giving you fair warning
Shaun: Is it gonna hurt?
Claire: Uhh, I'm not over budget but I have ordered furnishings for

all the bedrooms
Shaun: Good
Claire: It was fun. I had help from Tia, a local designer. She's invited me to a girls night out. She owns the café
Shaun: Making friends here, then?
Claire: I hope so
Shaun: Putting down roots?
Claire: I've only got a six-month visa, so not likely
Shaun: You'll have to marry a resident then, to stay
Claire: I'm looking every day
Shaun: Is that right?
Claire: Uh-huh... Vern tells me he's not interested
Shaun: He's playing hard to get
Claire: Y'think?
Shaun: Definitely
Claire: Oh well. And you're gay, so I'm running out of options

Shaun considered his response.

Shaun: I'm not gay, Claire

He felt his pulse racing as he waited for what she was going to say next.

Claire: You're not?
Shaun: You're shocked?
Claire: But... All the things I've said! Oh, SHIT! I'm SO Sorry!
Shaun: Woah. Slow down
Claire: I was only messing around; I wasn't flirting with you. Honest
Shaun: I know
Claire: I really like it here and you're my boss and I don't want to ruin things and now I'm so embarrassed and I'm going to meet you and it's all going to be super awkward and if you want to stop chatting, I totally understand
Shaun: Don't stress out. I don't want us to stop talking
Claire: You don't?

Shaun: No why would I? Do you?
Claire: No
Shaun: So are we cool?
Claire: Yeah. I guess. But I'm still cringing. I've said way too much. And I can't believe I told you about my naked swim
Shaun: You didn't
Claire Oh God
Shaun: You only said you were floating on top of the water
Claire: Ground swallow me up. Please. NOW!

He grinned at her embarrassment. He'd think about that swim of hers later. It was fun teasing her. Was it time to tell her? Not everything, but a little bit more.

Shaun: I had a long talk with Rawiri tonight. You remember the kid I was telling you about? The one who's working on the waka?
Claire: The canoe?
Shaun: We all went for a practice out on the water this evening and after, me and him had a bit of chat. Things are tough at home for him. I want to help if I can 'cos things haven't always been easy for me either
Claire: Can you help him?
Shaun: Honestly? I'm not sure. It's hard when you're in the middle of things. Things that you think are normal. But they aren't, and you can't see the bigger picture.
Claire: And Rawiri?
Shaun: He's still stuck in that groove. His dad's in a gang. He wouldn't say much but he's got that look about him like he's seen stuff no kid should be seeing.
Claire: You sound like you know a lot about this.
Shaun: I do. I spent years hiding from my dad. By the age of six, I could tell you what skin smells like when it's burned by a cigarette. And why you always keep your mouth shut about it.
Claire: Oh my... I'm so sorry, Shaun
Shaun: I packed it away. Buried it deep inside me and got on with life, as you do. Then one night a few months back, my past slammed

into me hard.

He took a deep breath. How much would he say?

Shaun: A woman I knew well, she'd spent years being abused by her husband and she opened up to me about it 'cos I saw her scars and, well, you can't kid a kidder, as they say.
Claire: Did you help her?
Shaun: Yeah, I did. She was sick, Claire. So sick, that she'd had enough. One night she came to see me. She'd defended herself and she'd killed him. And I covered it up for her so she wouldn't get arrested.

He held his head in his hands waiting for her reply, not daring to hope.

Claire: You did what you thought was right at the time
Shaun: And I don't regret it

He wondered what she'd say about that, but she had to know the truth. He was glad that he'd helped Maureen that night.

Claire: So, you're running too?
Shaun: Yes, I'm running too. I had to leave someone very special to me. And before you ask me the question I asked you, yes I did love her. I still do
Claire: And can you get in touch and tell her?
Shaun: Maybe, if she wants to find me

If only he could be there now. How he longed to wrap her in his arms. Feel her soft hair with his mouth, bring his lips down and trail them softly along her neck, kissing away all her sadness and anxieties.

His heart ached. Talking to Claire hurt more than the silence.

His thoughts were punctured by a knock on his door. It was late.

"Ari?"

Shaun got up from his bed, answering the door in his t-shirt and boxers.

"Michelle's called. The baby's coming. You good here?"

"Yeah, sweet."

Shaun touched his friend's arm.

"Good luck, mate."

My head is spinning as I try to process this. I can't sleep, everything he's written keeps running through my mind.

Helping a woman… Then why did he have to leave?

And then the realisation seeps into my thoughts. And the crushing truth of it.

Does *she know*?

I scroll quickly through to find the photo of him climbing the rock.

Studying it, I can tell now, the shape of his body. It's him. I'm almost certain of it. How could I not have known? Our conversations… our deep connection?

Now I see it, it's obvious.

And he's brought me here. And he loves me.

I can't help myself, even though it's way past midnight I click on the messaging app and type his name.

Claire: Sion?

My phone buzzes back in answer.

For the first time, a video call.

"You found me."

He's staring at me, his hair mussed up like he's been finding it as hard to sleep as me.

"You found me too."

But it's tears, not words that are flowing now.

"Shaun," I manage to stutter. "I'm so sorry I didn't believe you and didn't go with you that night. I was such a fool. I tried to call you but you'd gone. I've regretted it every single day."

"Claire!"

His voice cracks too and I can see that he's struggling to hold it together.

"I was so confused. Can you ever forgive me, Shaun?"

He sniffs.

"Yes. Of course. You're here now."

"Yes, I'm here."

"Please don't cry," he rasps, rubbing his face.

"They're happy tears."

I smile at his face on the screen and wipe the salty trickles away.

"I've missed you so much."

"Did you suspect?"

"No. But that bond we have, I've only ever had it with you. It was weird that me and Shaun had it too."

He chuckles lightly and sniffs, serious again.

"I didn't kill Glyn."

"Does Annie know her mother killed her father?"

"No. It was for Maureen to tell her not for me."

"I'll never breathe a word of it, Shaun. I promise."

Recovering himself too, he rakes his hand through his hair and looks straight at me. His blue eyes piercing my heart.

"I'm not proud of everything in my past, Claire, but I was always working for the good guys."

"Don't worry, Jason told me everything."

"My wingman."

He looks relieved and still emotional. We both are.

"I met more of the Scousers after you'd gone. They came after me in Greece."

"Jason told me. After that, I had to get you here."

"You? Of course. There was no job. And Jason was in on it?"

His eyes burn with intensity as I mull that over.

"I never meant to trick you, Claire. But I wasn't sure how you'd react if I contacted you."

"I'm really glad you did."

"You don't need to be afraid anymore. I'll protect you. You'll be safe here, with me."

His words make me ache for him.

"When will I see you?"

"Ari's wife's gone into labour. I'll need to stay until the end of term."

"I'm not going anywhere."

I can't say more. I can't tell him of how I'll be dreaming about the warmth of his lips as they gently cover mine or the shivers of anticipation that wash over me in waves as I imagine his hands softly feeling their way around my body in tentative exploration.

None of that can be spoken about yet.

"Sweet dreams, Shaun," I breathe, exhausted yet elated.

"You too, Claire," he whispers back before I end the call.

CHAPTER 15

---------*---------

The printed out photos lay flat on the desk in front of him. Several were of her with a friend on a wooden deck area at the front of a house. There was a good shot of her head. They'd used a telephoto lens and he could see her neck and make out the scar-line down it. It was her alright.

Irish leaned back in his chair and considered his next move. There was another woman with her, not Sion Edwards. That was disappointing. Was he going to waste time, effort and money chasing her down when the rat wasn't even there?

He needed more. He'd wired the five thousand through, so it wasn't unreasonable to ask.

He logged into the secure mailing account.

'*Cobra King,*

Is there a man with her? New to the area. Six foot. White. Welsh. If you can get me proof he's there, we'll talk more.
Irish.'

And if Sion Edwards was there? He felt a surge of excitement at the prospect.

Flicking through his contacts, he pressed the phone to call.

"Whitey? It's Irish."

He let him rattle on. Whitey was a big fan of his new white VW van.

He wasn't sure how this would play out, so it was softly, softly. Whitey was a hard nut. He'd chopped that scumbag into fish food even after he'd got his money back for him. But even so, he was still touchy as Hell about his dead twin brother. Even after thirty years.

"Listen la', I've got a favour to ask yer."

"D'ya still have little Vinny's birth certificate?... Does yer mam still keep everything in a box? *Ah!* Fair play to her... yeah... yeah... she *has* had it tough.` `

He yawned silently. Enough buttering him up.

"*Errr* Whitey? How hard would it be to get hold of it for us? The birth certificate? That's right... Just for a few days... Yeah... 'course we'd give her summat for it... A holiday?.... Go on then... She loves Prestatyn, does she?... I'm sure we can fix her up with a static caravan on the Welsh coast... For *a month*?"

Cheeky git.

"I need it by tomorrow... The Richmond? Alright. Two o'clock it is."

It was done.

At this stage it was only an idea. But things took time to organise, and as Vincent Cullen, Whitey's now not so dead twin brother, he'd be free to go wherever he wanted without the National Crime Agency keeping tabs on him.

Even to New Zealand.

When Shaun had agreed to help row the waka, he hadn't realised he'd be bare-chested and wearing a piupiu, which was a skirt made entirely of flax leaves. Thank God he'd been able to wear his black Speedo shorts under it.

He'd taken a selfie for Claire but she hadn't opened it yet.

And now, here he was, climbing into the waka with nineteen men.

The massive canoe was floating well. And Ari was beside him

too, in what he was coming to rapidly realise was far more than a boat launch.

Rawiri nodded to Shaun and they moved up into the back of the waka like they'd practised. He was certain he was only there to make up the muscle, but it was still a huge honour for him. He was being allowed to take part in something symbolic and spiritual. This was not purely a boat ride.

Blessings were given and the waka was named. The tradition, Ari told him, went way back to when the first iwis or tribes were named after their canoes.

Local families lined the estuary, willing them on. And then, as each man held his oar vertically to the sky, Ari stood up tall in the waka, proud and invincible in his ceremonial kākahu, a spectacular cloak of feathers.

Speaking in Māori he commanded the men and they flattened their oars. Touching the water with them they began to paddle as they'd practised. Together as one, they stroked out onto the tidal current and then worked steadily along the estuary.

In the distance, Shaun was aware of a buzz of cheering and shouting from the shore, but no more than that. The bank had become blurry in his peripheral vision as he focussed on his oar and the rhythm of the strokes. Feeling only the pride of the men flowing like electricity and powering their corded muscles, they paddled their new waka first up to and then back from the river's mouth.

And on the estuary headland, blending in amongst the crowds one woman watched them. Her heart burst too as she followed the wake of the waka as it sliced through the brown river water towards the sea.

Arriving back at the riverbank, Ari and Shaun jostled through the crowded shoreline surrounding the returned waka. Strangers slapped the backs of the waka captain and his Pākehā friend.

Rawiri pushed excitedly past them, and Shaun watched him heading towards a group of tough-looking tattooed men.

One of them stared back aggressively at Shaun and he glanced away. It was a proud day for the boy, but Rawiri's situation concerned Shaun.

Ari had told him to leave it be because Rawiri's dad was into some serious shit. They had plantations of skunk set up in a forestry unit. Shaun had seen marijuana growing wild around the lodge but he hadn't realised that criminal gangs were farming it out this way.

And would Rawiri get sucked in too? He couldn't save them all, but he vowed to talk to Rawiri again before he left.

Finally, they found a space in the crowd to stand and breathe easy. Ari put his hand on Shaun's shoulder.

"Hey, you're whanau now. Family."

Shaun swallowed a hard lump in his throat. How could Ari, new father and well-respected leader of men know what that meant to him? To be told he was 'family.'

He cleared his throat.

"Thanks, bro. You're only looking for a babysitter."

"There is that."

Michelle came over and Ari carefully took his new baby boy Kauri from her. Reaching forward, he passed the sleeping child over to Shaun who took him gently and held him.

"Seriously, thanks, man," Shaun said quietly, gazing at the sleeping child in his arms. "I will never forget today. And to be whanau with you. It means a lot. More than you know."

Ari looked him in the eye, commanding and displaying respect.

"I'm here for you, bro', even after our gig at the hostel's up."

"Me too, brother. I'm gonna miss you all."

"I'm expecting an invite over to yours, real soon," Ari laughed. "So, get the stubbies in, yeah. Might be sooner than ya think, if this little fulla keeps me awake much more."

Little Kauri looked so angelic, fast asleep in his arms. One week left, it was all he had until the students finished school and the hostel shut for good.

He was genuinely sorry to be leaving. He'd learned so much from the boys and from Ari. And there was so much that he admired about Ari's ways. Especially, how connected he was to his place. His environment, his culture, his family.

"Shaun."

He glanced up. Stunned.

She was standing there. In front of him.

Long, silky, dark hair sweeping down across one shoulder, full red lips, reflective aviators masking her eyes. Her long, black t-shirt dress was slit up the sides giving a hint of her fabulous legs.

His heart pounded.

"Claire."

She slipped her glasses onto the top of her head as they stood in awkward silence, unable to speak, both overwrought, unable to take their eyes off each other.

"Err... Claire. This is Ari."

"Ari, this is my friend who's looking for her father."

"Hi Ari," she smiled. "Thanks for your advice, though I've not made any enquiries yet."

Her eyes pulled back towards Shaun's bare chest.

It had been six months since he'd seen her but the physical magnetism between them took his breath away.

As did his sudden bout of shyness. For the first time in his life, he was stuck for words.

Ari stood transfixed, staring at her too, seemingly also unsure of what to say.

Looking away, Claire touched her neck nervously.

He plucked his son carefully from Shaun's oblivious arms.

"Kia Ora, Claire... *uh*, I think that this little one needs a change, so I'm gonna get outta here... See ya later at the hāngi, bro."

"Hāngi?" Claire asked, looking confused and a little disconcerted by Ari's reaction to her.

"They've got a heap of food cooking in this underground oven they've dug. You gotta see it," Shaun explained breathlessly, finally able to speak. "Did you see us?"

She repositioned her hair over her neck self-consciously.

"Yes... I got a picture too. The boat cutting through the morning mists. And your friend there, standing in the middle. I'll never forget it. Was it alright for me to come?"

"Claire!"

He took her hand, her almond eyes meeting his and lingering there. His bare skin goosebumped as he felt the charge between them.

Unable to bear the intensity any longer, she glanced shyly away.

He watched her trying desperately to recover her composure.

"It's more than alright."

She flicked him a nervous smile.

"Look at you. Let me see what you're wearing."

Shaun obliged by stepping back and turning slowly for her as she giggled.

She was still on edge, he could tell.

"What would they say in the Cross Keys if they could see you now?"

"Let's keep this to ourselves, eh?"

He took both of her hands and she gasped as he pulled her in towards him, her eyes widening with surprise but desire too as she gazed up at him.

His bare skin felt the warmth of her t-shirt dress and the softness of her breasts pressed up against him as he lowered his head down towards hers.

How much had he longed to kiss her? She had no idea. Or maybe she did? To put his lips on hers, hold her in his arms, feel her heart beating against his.

But not here.

Not where the boys and everyone could see them.

He grazed the top of her forehead gently with his mouth, and using every ounce of willpower he had, he released her hands, fixing them solidly on her shoulders.

"Wanna get outta here? I need to get changed."

Taking her hand in his, they walked back inland away from the headland of the estuary and the crowds, back towards the deserted beach and the school hostel.

She looked around at the closed-up wooden school buildings

and the hostel in front of them.

"So, this is where you're staying?"

The look she gave him crackled in the air between them. There was no way he could invite her in to see his room.

"Yip. Give me five minutes to change my skirt."

"Take your time. I'm fine out here, catching the rays. But be warned, if you come out in a dress, I'm walking away."

She sat down on the wall with her aviators back on.

Dammit! Did she have any idea of the effect she was having on him?

She brushed her hair over her shoulder again when she saw him coming back out. This time in shorts and a t-shirt.

"Better?"

"I preferred the bare chest."

She instantly coloured up.

Crossing the road from the school they dropped down onto the empty beach and found a spot to sit together on the sand.

She scooped up the fine sand in her hands and looked wistfully at the waves.

"My first New Zealand beach."

He leaned his head against her soft hair tumbling down over her shoulder.

"The first of many, I hope. How about when I finish up here, we take off and tour the country? The summer's nearly here, we could head over to the Bay of Islands and then down to the bubbling mud places and the mountains in the South. What d'you think?"

"Shaun."

Something was off. He tried to see her face but she'd turned her head away from him.

"You don't have to do this. Honest."

"What?"

He was confused.

"Claire, please?"

She twitched her neck.

"You don't have to be with me, because of this."

"Claire?"

He moved his arm to try and touch her face, to see her, but she flinched and he held off.

"Shaun, you're a decent guy. You feel bad about me. I get it."

Shaun rubbed his eyes and took a deep jagged breath, trying to quell all the emotions welling up inside. Love, hurt, fear, it all felt the same.

"Is that what you think?"

Turning her head to face his, her hand caressed his cheek.

"How would I ever stop worrying that I'm your charity case every time you look at me?"

She searched deep into his eyes.

Could she not see how he felt? How much he loved her?

Leaning tentatively towards her, his lips gently found hers and feathered across them and along her face.

"Is this charity?"

He nuzzled her ear with insistent kisses that sent her skywards.

"Or this?"

His hand carefully lifted her long silky tresses off her neck.

"Do you trust me to do this?" he breathed, his lips still on her ear.

She nodded.

Healing her with his mouth, his lips gently felt their way over her scar, brushing her skin, gently, coaxingly over her neck. Then, up along her defined jawline until his lips finally and tantalisingly found hers.

"Do you truly trust me, Claire?" he whispered, his lips against hers.

"Yes," she gasped.

He edged apart. His eyes hooded with desire.

"So, now you trust me, do you believe me when I say that I love you, Claire?"

He flicked a lock of her hair tenderly off her face.

"Not because of your wounds, or any sense of guilt or duty because the men were after me and you got hurt."

She let out a sob deep within and he answered it with a light kiss.

He cupped her face in both of his hands, his eyes meeting hers and burning with the passion he felt.

"I'm in love with you because you've gotten to be my best friend. And, if I'm being brutally honest, I fancy the pants off you. So much, it hurts."

She breathed out a small sigh. Her eyes still lost in his.

"Good answer."

Lifting her hands to his chest she pushed him gently back flat onto the sand.

Taking his mouth hungrily, she kissed him deeply, opening up to him as a tide of emotions flooded through her, drowning out all her doubts and fears.

Surprised, relieved, overjoyed he responded ravenously; their tongues becoming wrapped in delicious desire for each other as they became a torrid tangle in the sand.

The low pop-popping of a bike engine suddenly brought Claire to her senses.

"*Woah…*"

She pulled herself free from below him.

"I think we might be drawing an audience."

She giggled, drawing away from Shaun.

"Making out on the beach in broad daylight. See, they're taking photos of us."

Shaun turned around and then jumped up when he saw them.

"*Shit!* That's Rawiri,"

Three Harley Davidsons revved and pulled away, one with a boy on the back still dressed in his ceremonial clothes.

Shaun sidles up closer to me, shoulder to shoulder, his thigh touching mine as we sit on the grass, our bellies full of sweet potato and lamb from the hāngi.

We've been watching the girls perform with the poi. They're

like balls that they move about and spin as they sing. It's so clever and they're all so strikingly beautiful in their traditional woven dresses.

And it's been party-party all day after the waka launch and I don't want to go.

"I need to be heading, I don't want to be travelling back through the forest after dark."

He gives me a smouldering look that I'm finding impossible to resist. What is it about him? My body thrums as I feel him next to me. I think about our kiss on the beach, about him bare-chested. His tan, muscular body.

I clear my throat.

There are parents and kids everywhere, this is not the time or the place. And as much as my body aches to stay, I can't. It wouldn't be right to sneak into the hostel.

He stands up and offers me his hand.

"Walk you to the ute?"

We make our way out of the party and wander back towards the car park.

"It drives okay?"

"Yeah. Good choice."

He seems suddenly a little nervous too. And when I get out my car keys, I'm not sure either what to say beyond, *I can't keep my hands off you.* Or *I want you right now, here in the car park.*

So, I opt to say nothing and the silence becomes edgy between us, electrically charged.

He feels it too, I can tell.

My hand is on the truck's door.

"I better be off, then."

"Okay," he mumbles, "Call me when you get back."

I turn to open the door.

"Claire."

He sweeps me into his arms, his hand cradling the crook of my neck, his mouth tasting soft and sweet. A groan rumbles from deep within him as I feel the silky softness of his tousled hair and our tongues dance together in a hot, fiery kiss.

Feeling the flames building deep within me, my hands roam over his broad shoulders following the contours of his back and down onto that spectacularly muscular chest.

So much for Mr Nice. He presses me back against the door of the truck, kissing me intensely, passionately, ravenously. I feel his hardness against my stomach, and his hands under the slits of my dress, stroking their way up inside my thighs.

"Easy, soldier," I mumble, suddenly coming to my senses.

He pulls away suddenly and punches his fists into his trousers to stop himself from touching me. It's still broad daylight, but this time thankfully there's no one around.

"What is it with you?" he says shakily. "I'm sorry. I can't help myself. You do things to me."

I take a deep breath, feeling the unspent desire still pulsing through my core.

"I wish you could come back with me. I want you. All of you."

He rakes his hand through his hair.

"Me too. But I can't."

Ari's off duty and with the waka celebrations, a couple of the boys are staying over through the weekend.

"I guess, I'll see you at the lake lodge, then."

I get into the truck a little unsteadily.

"I can't wait," he says huskily, leaning into the ute and finding my lips for another toe-curling kiss.

"I love you, Claire."

I get lost in his hooded eyes; my heart thumping, my body aching for him.

"I love you too."

CHAPTER 16

---------*---------

"Bingo! Fuckin' Bingo! YES!"

The photos were undeniable.

Claire Williams. There she was, in the crowds talking to a bloke wearing a grass skirt. Then another one of her, this time snogging him. Then, and this was the hattrick in the back of the net, a full picture of the same bloke in shorts jumping up to look straight at the camera. And man, did he look pissed off.

Not as pissed off as he'd be when he saw his bird's head blown off in front of him, Irish sneered. The grass.

He lined the print up next to the only grainy picture he had of Sion Edwards from before.

There was no doubt it was the same bloke.

"Gotcha."

Cobra King was awaiting instructions. And money.

No problem his end with that.

The next part was all about timing. And he was looking forward to it. He'd never been to New Zealand.

Now his passport had come through, there were arrangements to be made.

He clicked online and checked flights.

'Cobra King,

Thank you for the photos. Excellent work, my friend. I'll be with you soon. I'll pay you to pick them up and keep them for me. Alive.

Are there any abattoirs near you? There's a debt that needs to be repaid.

Irish'

◆ ◆ ◆

As I walk through into the café's garden terrace, Tia gets up from a crowded table and comes over to me. Holding my hand, she introduces me to her friends.

An empty champagne flute is quickly sent my way and one of her friends offers me a drink of the pink fizz they're drinking.

"I'm driving."

"Pfft," Tia dismisses, "You can crash at mine."

There's no excuse and my arm's easily twisted. To be honest, I've been aching to see Shaun so badly I can hardly bear to be at the lake this week. I've been about to jump into the ute and head back up north to him three times at least, and it's only Monday. A night away will be a welcome distraction.

"Claire's a Pom. She's moved into Jake's Place out at the lake."

"No way! Look at you."

Aroha, one of the friends, looks me up and down. I squirm as I feel her eyes on my neck.

"You're whanau."

Tia tuts at her.

"Jees, she's only just got here. Don't scare her away."

We order food and more pink fizz, which is going down far too fast. And pretty soon we're all laughing and joking. Tia offers me a job working in the café and I've had more invitations to things that are going on than I will ever remember once I've sobered up.

I tell them about my weekend; the waka and Shaun. And they laugh at my pronunciations and ways of describing stuff.

"You're so Māori, girl. I mean it. Seriously."

"D'ya think?"

My skin's more or less the same tone as theirs. My hair's like theirs too, thick and dark. My eyes study their features, as well as they can after a few glasses of bubbles.

"My dad's from New Zealand."

"How?"

"He was a rugby player. My mum said it was a one-night thing. She never talked about it. His name on the birth certificate is all I've got."

"And your neck?"

I shudder when they raise it, but I've had too much wine at this point and I don't care anymore. Shaun tells me I'm still beautiful.

"A guy put a knife to me and I fought him off."

"What happened to him?"

"Prison."

"So, you're a regular warrior too."

I giggle.

"Yeah, whatever."

"You should get a moko over it."

"A moko?'

"Yeah."

Tia scrolls through images on her phone, showing me the traditionally dressed Māori women with black tattooed lips and thick black grooving lines curling across their chins.

My eyes widen and they howl with laughter.

"Is this like some distraction theory? Tattoo my face and they won't notice my neck?"

When we've calmed down, Aroha stands and rolls up her shirt at the back to show me a huge tribal design tattooed right across it. It looks super-cool, I have to admit.

"There's still no way I'm tattooing my chin."

"Not your chin, ya wally. Down ya neck. It'd be cool as."

"No way. My friend got a tattoo to cover a scar on her shoulder. You'd need to be pretty brave to have one down your neck."

"I guess, but at least you'd wear it as art, not twitch every time someone looks your way."

"I'm not doing that, am I?"

Tia fills my glass. Their faces are enough to confirm that there's no way I can argue the point.

"I missed you last night."

Shaun had finally got through to Claire. She'd texted him regularly but with her going out on Monday and the farewell activities going on in the hostel, they hadn't managed to video chat for a few days.

"Yeah, sorry about that. I ended up staying out at the beach with Tia and my phone went flat," Claire said relaxing back flat on the bed.

"It's been a mad forty-eight hours but I've met so many people."

"Sounds as if you've been having fun."

"I have. I love that big beach, it's so wild out there."

"And it goes on for miles. I did some kite fishing on it with Frank."

"Catch anything?"

Claire sniggered.

"Hey! My fishing's got a lot better since then."

"Tia introduced me to her family and friends, and she says we're whanau. D'you think I look Māori?"

"Yeah, you do."

"Cool. She's going to help me find my dad. Every time I said his name she was rolling over in stitches, so I promised to text it to her. Oh, and she thinks I should get a moko."

"A what?"

"A traditional tattoo. Women get tattooed on their chin. She thinks I should get one like that down my neck."

He touched his arm subconsciously. The large Welsh plumes of his regiment emblem across his bicep covered over previous inked-in scratchings, battle wounds from his time as a teenager in residential care.

"Is that what you want?"

"What d'you think?"

"I think getting a tattoo on your neck's a bit like having a kid."

"*Eh?*"

"You've gotta be fully committed to it. Once it's on, it's there for life."

"Yeah, there is that."

She yawned.

"Sorry!"

"Tired?"

"Last night was a late one. We had a bonfire on the beach."

He was suddenly serious.

"Would the tattoo help you be less self-conscious about your scar?"

He could see her nose screw up.

"Hey, Shaun. Don't worry. I'm not getting a tattoo down my neck."

She looked intently at the screen.

"But you know what? I have decided something. Let them stare. I don't care anymore about my scar. It's part of my story. Who I am."

Shaun laughed, a little relieved.

"When I see your scar, I see your bravery."

"You do?"

"Yeah. Makes you even more beautiful. And I think I proved last weekend what effect you have on me."

She stared wickedly at the screen and into his eyes.

"You mean, what I felt pressed up against me?"

"My days undercover are over, so it definitely wasn't a gun. It could have been the waka though? Hidden in my shorts."

Claire let out a loud laugh.

"The optimism of men. You'll make a fisherman yet."

Shaun cleared his throat.

"Claire, when I come home on Friday, we can take this as slow as you want. Stay friends, even. It'd kill me, but I never want you to feel pressured."

She was studying him through the video link.

"Hmm, let's see how it goes, yeah? I mean, I'm finding it really hard not to think about it."

He saw her suddenly flush red. He loved that nervous innocence about her, naive and sexy at the same time.

"I mean '*you.*' Not to think about *you*. I think about you, most of the day, actually."

"You do?"

"I wish I was with you now. I'll be dreaming about you, Claire"

"Me too."

She gave him an impish grin.

"I'll show you Friday what we did."

I wake up ridiculously early, my stomach filled with butterflies. My heart racing. Shaun's coming home.

And then, a moment of cavernous dread. What on earth am I going to wear?

I look at my small selection of worn-out clothes and well-travelled underwear. It was all I could carry in my rucksack, but now after months on the road and what with the painting and manual work, it's all gone a bit tatty.

That's it, I decide. The girl needs to shop. And fast. It's a two-hour drive over to the east coast, but Tia said that there are decent stores there. Whatever they have, it's got to be an improvement on the checked farmer shirts and armpit-hugging granny knickers in town.

I get there as the shops are opening and pull up by the marina where the town's harbour inlet is lined with expensive yachts in their moorings. Tia was right when she told me that the east coast was a world away from the agricultural backwaters and wild, forested west side of the country.

Fuelled by a quick coffee and croissant in the morning sunshine I go in search of some serious retail therapy.

By early afternoon I'm shopped out and heading back on the

long drive to the lake.

My hair's styled and I'm waxed and polished like a showroom car. I'm feeling great, but those pesky little butterflies of anticipation are still there. And their wings beat like mad when I try to decide which of the lingerie sets on the seat beside me I'm going to wear tonight.

"That you ready for home?"

Ari was emptying the last remnants of the large fridge as Shaun lugged his bags through to the kitchen.

He'd spent all day with his friend, cleaning and stripping down the hostel after the boys left that morning for their summer holidays.

It was strange to think that the hostel wouldn't be opening up again.

"I'm gonna miss this place. And the boys."

"You did good, Shaun."

"Thanks, bro. I'm still worried about Rawiri, though."

He'd not been back to school or the hostel since Shaun had seen him heading off on the back of the motorbike.

Ari scratched his head.

"His mum's related to a cousin of mine. I'll find out what's goin' on with him. But from the sounds of it, he's headed to the forest camp with his dad."

That was what Shaun feared too. He put his hand on Ari's shoulder.

"All the best with your teaching course. Give my love to Michelle."

"And to Claire."

Ari snuck him a look that cracked Shaun's smirk into a broad cheesy smile. Ari hadn't left him be until he'd spilled the beans about Claire.

Ari had been curious. He'd wanted to know everything about her. Who she was, how they'd met, what she'd been doing in

Wales before she came out to New Zealand. Who she thought her dad was. Shaun had told him everything about her, even about the attack. He was going to miss his friend.

"See you at the lodge. Soon, yeah? There's room for you all and plenty of trout in the lake."

"Still will be while you're fishing there."

Ari squared and faced his friend, grasping his hand and leaning in, nose to nose with Shaun in the traditional hongi.

"Ka kite anō. See you soon, bro."

CHAPTER 17

---------✶---------

Something was off.

He could see something was wrong as soon as he turned the bend after the public beach. The ute had been left with the driver door wide open and the place looked deserted. The lodge appeared to be locked up and there was nobody about.

Shaun slowed the BMW right down.

Then, as he rolled the car warily up towards the lodge, he clocked the full bags of groceries strewn across the passenger seat of the truck. His stomach lurched. That wasn't right at all.

A part of his brain he'd hoped he'd never have to use again, began firing up, quickly assessing the situation.

It didn't matter which way he evaluated it. It wasn't good.

And where was Claire?

Edgily, he turned the steering wheel, cruising closer, scanning his eyes over the property and across towards the barn. Slowly circling in the turning space before the driveway to the house, he headed back towards the public beach area. He turned there and then parked up on the grassy verge by the track to the lodge.

From there, he surveyed the lodge and the drive meticulously. At first from inside the car and then outside from the cover of the car door.

Was there someone there? There were no movements, no un-explained shadows from the buildings or inside the windows of the lodge. But he was still a little too far away to be sure.

Bursting from behind the car, his trainers slid in the dust as he power-sprinted up the track and over towards the property. He dived for cover behind a thick line of flax bushes a few metres before the barn.

No explosions of splintering wood, no popping bangs. Everywhere remained ghostly still.

Taking his chance he lunged himself forward into the open once more, bounding forward to the edge of the barn wall and then making a final dash to the barn door.

Yanking it open he scanned the space with his eyes, then slid swiftly inside and gathered his breath.

Think.

What had happened here?

Think.

He rubbed his face, trying to calm himself down.

The barn was spookily silent. Motes of dust suspended on the cool air inside. It had been swept clean. Gardening tools had been neatly propped up on one side.

He examined the space and checked the second storage area which he'd left open.

Nothing looked disturbed. Everything was tidy. There were no signs of any struggle.

He checked the top loft area, hidden from view. If he was hiding, he'd choose there. Out of view, secret and only accessible by ladder.

But it was empty. The old mattress, the tilly lamp and stove; it looked the same as before.

His heart sank.

She hadn't been here either.

Grabbing a kindling axe that was propped up in the corner, he scooted back towards the barn door and spied back out from behind it again.

He'd developed catlike senses in the special forces, and he was certain now that he couldn't sense anyone else around. But, what he'd give right now for a semi-automatic.

Warily, hatchet in hand and tracking the edge of the barn he ducked low as he moved. Then he broke out into the open, sprinting towards the ute.

Diving for cover behind the truck's open door, he crouched there for a minute. And more. Waiting, in case it was a trap.

He exhaled.

Gingerly, he straightened a little and took one more cautious assessment of the area before turning his attention to the ute.

Car keys lay discarded in the dust two feet away from the driver's side.

He picked them up.

"Claire, honey," he whispered as much to himself as to her.

"Where are you?"

The house looked like it was locked up.

A large unopened parcel lay propped up, undisturbed against the kitchen door.

This was no home invasion.

Leaning his head inside, tentatively he began searching inside the cab.

His gut churned.

Three bags of new clothes and one of beautiful lingerie.

As he lifted out a pair of aubergine-coloured panties and felt their soft satin in his fingers, his eyes began to sting and he let out a shaky breath.

Her handbag was still lying on the passenger seat.

He lifted it and looked inside. Her purse was still in there. Cash and bank cards untouched.

Growing a little bolder, he skirted around the truck door and felt the car's bonnet, then doubled back and released the catch from inside the truck and felt the engine underneath the bonnet.

Stone cold.

He examined the groceries. The chicken breasts she'd bought felt warm to touch in their cellophane and gave off an unmistakable whiff when he peeled back the wrapping.

On a hot day like this, she'd have had the air con on when she drove from Dargarei, he rationalised. It was early evening now so the shopping had to have been sitting in the sun for one, maybe two hours?

He stood up straight and surveyed the area thoroughly one more time.

More certain now that he was alone, he jogged over to the porch and tried the handle.

He was right, the place was still locked up.

Inside was tidy. No broken windows or damage to the lodge. No torn clothes. No pools of blood, thank God. He doubted she'd even made it inside.

Where was she?

"Claire!"

He called out her name loudly from the porch step, scanning carefully around, already feeling the futility of his cries.

His voice thickened.

"Claire? Are you there?"

But the only calls that answered him were the melodious songs of the tui birds in the trees and the flat-sounding squawk of Rowdy in the chicken coop.

"Claire!.... No!.... Fuck, no!"

He broke down.

They'd taken his Claire.

He willed himself to be the soldier he was. To think fast and hard. Be logical and analytical, think dispassionately about this.

Instead, he retched into the dirt in front of the house, his stomach desperately heaving up his anxiety and dread.

He wiped his face with the back of his hand and went over to kneel down at the lakeshore, cleaning his hands and splashing his face with water.

Who would have taken her?

There was a contract out on him, the officer from the British Consulate had confirmed that. And Claire had told him about the Scousers coming after her in Greece and the warning she'd been given.

His mind slammed back to a time before, when he'd been

grabbed by the Scouser gang. Irish had set a trap for him in a crowded boozer, where he'd been jumped by some goons and thrown into the boot of a car. It was highly unlikely that Irish would be able to do that here. And from what he'd seen of the Scousers, they weren't trained military men. They depended heavily on loyal gym-built meatheads.

Then, there was Jake's diary. That proved there were plenty of chancers in these parts too. Lowlifes scanning the dark web in search of a few easy bucks.

He checked the car over again. For something, anything that might be a clue. The seats. The footwell. The boot. The dirt around the car. He couldn't see any discarded cartridge casings. No guns had been fired as far as he could determine.

She'd been taken. He was sure of that. And she'd been taken alive.

He prayed that she'd not been harmed.

But if Claire was the target, why now? What had changed? The Scousers could easily have grabbed her in Greece.

His stomach knotted as it hit him.

Claire was being watched all along. She'd unwittingly led them to him. The bikers taking photos of them on the beach. It was the only time he'd met Claire.

There was only one course of action to be taken. He had to get Claire from wherever she was being held. Even if it meant taking the bullet himself.

His hand reached down to something in the dust below the porch. The used filter from a smoked roll-up.

Claire wasn't a smoker.

He put the butt to his nose and inhaled the sweet, cloying smell of marijuana.

The diary was evidence that the biker gang had gone after contracts at least once before. It had to be them. The Cobras.

Shaun grabbed his phone.

"Ari?"

He cut short his friend's quip that he was missing him already.

"Listen, mate, Claire's been abducted. I need directions to the

Cobra camp in the forest. Can you help me?"

CHAPTER 18

---------*---------

A bead of sweat runs down onto my lips and I taste its saltiness. My tears are dry now and my throat is parched. It's so suffocatingly hot in here.

The light coming in between the rotting slats is fading. Soon it will be pitch black in this wooden sweatbox. I try not to think about that, it's claustrophobic enough.

I try also to block out the stinging pain, pins and needles fizzing through my fingers. They're hot and swollen from the tight binding of the tape.

At the start, I tried shouting. Then I begged them for help. I pleaded that my hands were hurting and I needed water. But all I got was a rough kick to the side of the shed that cracked one of the rotten wood walls. That was followed by a blunt warning to shut the fuck up with the noise or they'd cut my tongue out.

I've not made a sound since.

I'm so angry with myself that I hadn't seen them. But they'd hidden their truck out of sight.

My head was full of things that seem so silly now. What I was going to cook for Shaun. Which of the new dresses I was going to wear. And whether to go for the classic satin lingerie or the more scanty, daring lacey set I'd bought.

I remember unhooking my belt and I was leaning across the seat for my handbag when they sprang me.

For big guys, they were real fast. They yanked the door wide open. A huge fist came slamming down over the keys, flinging them away before I could start up the engine.

Then he was grabbing me, tearing me from my seat. His friend behind him backing him up, ripping me roughly out of the ute and flinging me down onto the dirt.

There was no point in fighting. A third dude was pointing a gun at my head and his mean eyes told me he'd use it too. They bound my hands brutally tight with gaffer tape and hauled me into the back of their truck.

And here I am. At the place they call 'the camp.' From what I can see the place is an old horticultural unit in a clearing in the woods. We're not that far from the lodge, but we're deep down a maze of tracks in a thick jungly forest.

We parked up by a small scruffy wooden house where the men are living. It's a mess. Beer cans and bottles scattered everywhere. They're not into recycling. And there are rows of shiny chrome motorbikes. Harleys, choppers, serious big bikes. They look to me like an outlawed biker gang. Probably worse. It's definitely not tomatoes they're growing in the polytunnels, that's for sure.

Across the front of the house, they've hung a massive flag. At the centre is a hissing snake. Above it the words 'The Cobras' are written large in a graffiti-type font. It's the same design as on the photographer's jacket that day. They've been watching me for a while.

I got dragged out of the truck, then two mean-looking men marched me at gunpoint past two of the polytunnels to a row of homemade sheds where they keep their dogs.

They've shoved into the one at the end. The only one with a wooden door instead of chicken wire. I think they've jammed the door with something on the outside because I didn't hear a lock or a bolt. But whatever it is, it's heavy. My shoulder can't budge it.

The shed is cramped, it stinks of dog and it's as hot as Hell.

I try to comfort myself that they've not killed me yet. But, I'm not deluding myself, this has to be about Shaun. They're keeping me alive to draw him here.

Every so often, I hear men's voices floating around me. And the odd motorcycle engine noise approaching and then cutting out. There are dogs too, with low loud deep barks real close to me. They sound big and dangerous. I can hear them sniffing, scratching and moving about in the next box. And every so often one of them gives off a low menacing growl that I'm sure is directed at me.

"Rawiri? What you doing out at the lake?"

"Ari sent me. He asked me to take you to the camp."

Shaun frowned.

"You could get killed for this."

Rawiri shrugged it off.

"Yeah. And?"

"*And...* I can't let you do it."

"Too late, bro. I've already raxed their quad bike."

Shaun rubbed his cheek. When he'd asked his friend for directions, he hadn't meant for the kid to get wrapped up in it too.

"Go back."

Rawiri smirked.

"Give you a ride there, then?"

The boy wasn't giving up.

Shaun blew out a breath.

"Alright. Gimme a minute."

He dashed back into the kitchen and opened the freezer. At the bottom were two whole trout that Frank had caught.

He grabbed the small rucksack he'd already packed with useful gear while he was waiting for Ari's call back. His small pair of binoculars, an energy bar, water, a pair of pliers, gaffer tape, a kitchen knife. And on his shin under his cargo pants, he'd taped a small screwdriver and his penknife. It was an old trick but one that had saved his life before.

He reached for his fishing rod, passing the parcel which now lay open by the door. Five large canvas prints of the lake. Photographs taken by Claire.

He breathed deeply to force down all the pain and fear he felt and pushed past them back to Rawiri who was waiting for him on the quad bike.

"Tell them you've been at the lake."

Rawiri grinned, placing the rod between his legs and fastening the plastic bag of fish to the handlebars as Shaun sprang onto the back.

He patted the boy's shoulder.

"Thank you, my friend."

Together they took off, along the dusty track in the dusk back towards the main road.

After a few minutes on the tarmac of the highway, Rawiri slowed. Then without warning, they turned off the road into the bush, bouncing over the rough grass through a break in the wire fence. It was no more than a bunny run, a tyre-tracked clearing into the forest.

But then, Rawiri soon turned sharply again and Shaun could see the track becoming clearer and wider as the forest became thicker, closing off the last drops of daylight.

Shaun touched his shoulder.

"Stop."

Shaun hopped off and picked up two branches off the forest floor, placing them in a cross to mark the exit point.

"I need to find my way back outta here."

Rawiri switched the quad lights full on and they carried on, deeper into the forest.

Four more times they stopped. At each fork, Shaun hauled branches across the wrong track.

Finally, along a straight piece, it was Rawiri's turn to pull up.

"The camp's not far from here. Around the bend, then a quarter of a k at the end of the road."

They heard a dog starting to bark.

Shaun hopped off the back.

"I'll see what I can do about them bloody dogs."

"Appreciate it."

"The chick's in the first dog shed behind the polys. The one with the wooden door. Good luck, bro."

"Gonna need it, mate,"

Shaun flashed Rawiri a cocky smile though he felt far from confident inside.

The boy turned to move off.

"Hey, Rawiri?"

"Ah, yeah?"

The boy glanced back around at Shaun.

"What you've done for me. It was very brave. I'm proud of you."

Rawiri nodded a little sheepishly and sped off with his new rod and the bag of defrosting fish.

My pulse races. I can hear footsteps outside. They're coming closer. I bunch up into a ball in the corner at the rear of the shed as I hear them right by the shed.

Then, something heavy is moved off the door and it swings open in front of me in the half-light.

From the shadow filling the space where the door was, I can see it's another bald biker. It's too dark to see him properly, but this one is a monster of a man. He's massive.

He shines the torch from a mobile phone over me huddled up in the farthest corner.

Bending right down, he steps inside the shed. It's a squeeze for his huge, square shoulders through the door.

In his other hand is a plate of food and a plastic bottle. It looks like some kind of stew with a hunk of bread on the side. He sets it down like he's feeding a dog and then throws the plastic bottle of water after it, towards me.

"I need to pee."

I sound bolshy but I'm past caring.

I can feel his eyes on me, no doubt looking at the pitiful creature in front of him. Without words, he beckons at me with his head to get up and follow him.

I stagger forward past the plate of food and come out of the shed into the cool evening air.

"You can go over there."

"Shut ya yapping!" he snarls at the hysterical hounds. And they fall instantly silent.

"Can you untie me? I won't escape."

Something tells me to stand tall and I hold my head high in defiance, my eyes challenging his in the dusk.

"My circulation's gone and I can't feel my hands."

He stares down at me and I quell the gasp of fright as the moonlight reveals his densely tattooed face. Thick blue lines cover his nose then fan out over his forehead and extend in sweeping arches around his mouth swirling into bold circles across his cheeks. He's terrifying.

His mouth curves at my mock-bravery. Pulling out a blade from his back pocket, he slashes open the tape, freeing up my hands.

"Try to run and you're dead."

I lift my chin proudly and walk to a spot by the side of the shed. He turns his head as I squat.

Pulling up my jeans, I stumble my way back into the kennel, rubbing the circulation back into my hands.

"Thank you."

He slams the door shut behind me and it goes dark again.

"How the Hell did you get into this shit?" I hear him mutter outside the door.

Perhaps to himself? Perhaps to me?

Shaun veered towards the bushes at the side of the track. He started to jog as quietly he could, making contact with the ground on his midfoot, limiting the force, keeping his posture straight. Efficient soft running, like he'd been trained to do all those years ago.

A bright moon had risen, and as he approached the end of the track the forest was thinning out revealing the camp below him. It lay in a meadow with a stream running through it, a natural clearing in the woods.

He crouched down and slid onto his belly.

Retrieving the small pair of binoculars from his bag, he could see the layout of the buildings. First, a house with lots of motorcycles parked up. Choppers and custom bikes. There was a muscle truck there too, modified with jacked-up wheels. These guys liked to do a bit of showing off.

Like Rawiri had said, there were makeshift sheds at the back, behind the polytunnels.

It was a bad place to be. Behind the house. By the dogs.

Swiftly and silently he slipped down towards the camp gate. There, he deposited his rucksack in the irrigation trench that ran by the side of the gate following the fence. He covered it in the long grass.

Then he crept stealthily into the compound, staying in the shadows and heading through the motorcycles towards the polytunnels and the sheds beyond.

An explosive shout. And then another.

Shaun crouched low behind a modified Fatboy. The shouts were coming from the house.

Rawiri's quad bike was parked up to the side by the door. It was likely that he was inside with them. Taking the heat because of him.

He weighed it up.

He should get Claire first. But, *dammit!* There was no way either that he could leave the boy if he was in some kind of strife.

He crawled around the motorcycles until he was safely under the back window, as close to the shouting as he could get without being seen.

"So you nicked my fuckin' quad, did ya? Ya little shit!"

An aggressive male voice, a little high-pitched. Angry. Then Rawiri.

"Didn't know it was yours, Jon."

"Well you do now. And nobody takes it without askin'. Not never!"

Shaun placed his ear under the windowpane, listening intently.

"Where you been, boy?"

A different voice this time. Deep and rumbling. Dangerous.

"The lakes. Fancied givin' my new rod a go."

Rawiri sounded upbeat. Cool. He was holding up well.

"Sure it wasn't the Antarctic?"

They'd felt the fish.

"Water was bloody cold, alright."

"That so?"

"Yeah."

Shaun heard the note of defiance in the boy's voice.

"You don't take the quad without askin' first, ya hear me?"

The tone was commanding but the words were a climb-down.

"Sorry, King."

"That all yer gonna say?"

The angry goat-voice again.

"Yes!" the deep voice thundered. "That is all I'm gonna fuckin' say. Unless you have a problem with that? *Or with me?*"

There was no debate after that. Rawiri was off the hook. For now.

Shaun moved swiftly away from the house towards the densely vegetated polytunnels.

There was no mistaking the jagged leaf of the large plants. Marijuana. Probably hydroponically grown. The high THC psychoactive looney toons variety that was in global demand.

He moved forward cautiously, past the end of the polytunnels stepping closer to the sheds.

Then froze.

A dog started up.

Shaun kept rigidly still.

Quickly realising that the others weren't joining in, the dog wound down and gave up.

Now was his chance and he needed to be quick. He sped forward again, running over the open ground towards the sheds fifty metres in front of him.

Shit!

He snagged his foot on something. It nearly sent him flying.

Two temporary security arc lights flickered, and then suddenly the ground around him lit up like it was day again. He was bathed in brilliant white light.

He groaned as he saw the fishing line snagged in his trainers. A homemade sensor. He hadn't expected that.

All the dogs were jumping now. Slavering and barking into a furious snarling crescendo. Winding themselves up like an air raid siren into a cacophony of gnashing and growling against the mesh doors of their kennels next to Claire.

This was his only chance. He needed to grab it now.

"Claire!"

"I'm in here."

His eyes darted to the end shed. It had a full wooden door barred across with a heavy wooden block.

No time to think.

He sprinted over and began lifting the solid block out of the way.

The door swung open and Claire flung herself into his arms.

"Shaun!"

He held onto her tightly as the air around them filled with the loud clicks of gun barrels being locked and loaded.

"Hey, King! We snagged ourselves a bite."

Ten armed men spread out in a circle around them stepped menacingly closer. With hands pointing upwards into the air and his back to his new guests, Shaun was roughly shoved with the end of a shotgun down onto his knees.

"Sion Edwards?"

"I'm Shaun Cobain."

"Whatever."

With a kick of a boot, he was forced into the kennel with Claire. The door jammed into place behind them.

"What'll happen to him?"

Shaun heard Rawiri's voice outside the door.

"Some Pom's coming," a deeper voice answered. "Wanted to cut them up at the meat plant. King told him he could either put a bullet in their skulls or piss off home."

"I'm so sorry, Claire."

It was all Shaun could say. He was such an idiot. He should have known that it was all too easy, that they would have booby-trapped the place.

Whatever had happened his brain had gone soft. He'd taken too many risks, been too careless. Now, they were both in deep trouble and it was his fault. Again.

"Shhh."

Claire comforted him, finding his lips with hers.

"One way or another you were always going to snag their line."

He kissed her again, this time more deeply, more passionately as if this kiss would be their last.

His mouth travelled from her lips towards the neckline of her scooped t-shirt. The little gasp she made set him on fire, and his hands found themselves underneath her top wandering their way upwards towards those wonderful breasts of hers.

Dammit!

He pulled himself reluctantly away from her.

"Sorry, Claire. I can't stop myself from touching you."

She leaned her forehead against his chest, her breathing thick with lust too.

God! What he'd like to do right now.

"You heard them? We're both gonna die anyway."

Shaun groaned.

"You're killing me too, you know that? We've gotta get out of here, even if it's only so I can make love to you properly."

Claire whispered into his ear, "I might have found a way."

CHAPTER 19

--------*--------

It was three a.m. and Shaun brushed Claire's head with his lips as she slept. Her head was lying gently against his chest, their backs propped against the wooden sidewall.

He stroked her hair. This wasn't how he'd imagined their first night together. And God knows he'd thought about it enough times.

Stirring, she came too.

"It's time," he mouthed.

He tried to spy out of the crack in the door but in the darkness, there wasn't much to see. The door was jammed fast, held firm by the block on the outside.

But Claire had already found another way. Two of the back wall wooden panels were pretty rotten. And with the help of the screwdriver and the penknife that were strapped to Shaun's leg they'd managed to get enough purchase on the rotten edges to lever them loose. It had been a painstakingly slow task to do quietly without the dogs starting up or the men who'd been walking around hearing them, but he was certain it would work.

Together they worked carefully now, in the dead of night, shifting the two loosened boards free and placing them softly onto the ground.

The tiny noises caused a snuffling next to them, but the dogs had got used to their scratchings and soon settled back down.

He could hear the rain drumming down onto the shed roof. It sounded like it was coming down hard.

"You ready?"

She nodded.

Shaun went first, squeezing through the gap and lifting himself up by the side of the shed to check.

After the hot box, the heavy rain on his face felt delicious, although he knew they'd soon be soaked.

The camp was deathly quiet.

Stretching his hand back into the gap, he helped Claire out into the wet, dark night. She took in deep breaths too, cooling herself then moving with him. Gingerly, they crept to the front of the shed.

Discarded on the ground beside the front door was the familiar plastic bag. Inside, the two defrosted trout. Rawiri?

Whoever it was, the fish would do nicely.

Alert to the tiniest sounds, the hounds had already started moving about and he heard the familiar whine of a dog stretching and yawning awake. In a few seconds, they'd start yapping.

Shaun grabbed the slippery trout and using his knife he cut the fish into pieces, tossing them into the cages for the dogs.

"Watch out for wires."

In the darkness he plotted their course to the polytunnels, stopping and pushing the screwdriver out into the grass in front of them, meticulously checking for wire. He treated it like a minefield. Getting caught meant certain death.

Claire followed close behind in careful, synchronised steps.

At the house they paused. There were no guards to be seen. Everyone appeared to be fast asleep.

Gesturing, Shaun counted them down with his fingers and they sprinted again. Keeping low they moved between the parked-up motorcycles and then ran clear, through the compound, before diving into the irrigation ditch by the gate for cover.

He looked back.

No lights had come on. The house remained in darkness, the dogs silent.

Feeling with his hands through the grass, he located his rucksack. Taking the quad would have been too risky.

"We're gonna need to leg it from here."

"How long've we got?".

"Three, four hours head start."

"That all? You haven't got any more handy tools taped onto your leg by any chance, have ya?"

"No, sorry. Only a pair of pliers in the rucksack. In case I needed to cut a fence."

She kissed him on the lips.

"My hero."

"What you doing? We gotta go."

But Claire was on her feet already, climbing out of the irrigation ditch. Droplets of rain ran down her arms and her hair and vest top were soaked through.

"Start running."

"Claire!"

She put her finger to her lips.

"Shh. Your turn to trust me."

She turned her heels and began heading back towards the house. Shaun looked torn

Putting his arms through the rucksack, he didn't want to leave her but what choice did he have after she'd said that to him?

Reluctantly he started a slow, leisurely jog.

In a few short seconds, Claire was back beside the motorbikes.

Soundlessly she went around each one in turn, finding the spark plug on the top of the cylinder head and snipping off the lead. In a few minutes, she'd managed to disable all but three Harleys. They were parked up close to the polytunnels on the other side of the house. Too close to the dogs.

With her pockets full, she spun on her heels and headed off to catch up with Shaun.

"Thank God!" he whispered to himself as he heard the sound of her feet pounding the ground behind him.

She pulled the plastic leads out from her pockets and cast them into the darkness beside her.

"It'll buy us a bit more time."

"Where do you learn to do that?"

She moved alongside him, jogging at a steady pace.

"Motor vehicle class. They packed the naughty ones off to college once a week."

He shot her a quirky look that sent her heart racing.

"Clever bad girl."

Quietly, they jogged the track, moving fluidly. Claire had been running most days and she was keeping up easily. The adrenaline and their fate, if caught, spurred them both on deeper into the forest.

"Want a breather?"

The rain had eased off and they'd passed three of his five markers, making good time although the dawn was starting to break now.

Claire bent over and took her breath.

"Let's carry on, I never want to go back there. And I don't fancy being cut up and turned into sausages."

Shaun agreed.

Jogging gently and steadily they found the final marker, turning them across the last much rougher section towards the main road.

"*Oww!*"

Shaun heard Claire's gasp and then an expletive behind him.

He turned around. She was flat, face-planted to the forest floor.

"It's alright."

She got back up and started walking, but Shaun could see she was in pain.

"Let's rest up for a minute or two."

"No bloody way. Come on."

She kept on walking determinedly through the pain, but he could see their progress was slowing up. She was hardly putting any weight on her foot and when he wasn't watching she was limping quite badly.

He checked his watch. It was after six. They'd be awake soon and then all Hell would break loose.

"Claire, we're nearly at the main road. We're gonna find a spot there and hide in the bushes."

Her ankle must have hurt because she didn't look like she was going to argue with him.

The main road loomed up on them before they knew it. Shaun saw the bend in the road a hundred metres in front of them. Behind them lay a good open stretch of road heading up towards the north.

"We're going to hide over there," he pointed.

At the side of the road, as was common in these parts, a deep irrigation ditch ran parallel to the road. Dense clumps of wild lily of the valley growing along it filled the air with a heady, heavenly perfume.

"Okay, this'll do."

It was deep, and with some branches to cover them, they'd be hidden from the road.

Taking her hand, Shaun carefully helped her down.

She sat and rested her ankle as he crossed the road back into the forest.

"Bushcraft."

With his penknife, he'd cut down an armful of large tree fern branches. He then built them a rudimentary hide.

Claire sat beneath their fern shelter slowly drying out whilst Shaun lay against the ditch, keeping a watch out for vehicles through his binoculars.

"Hey, there's one coming now."

A wagon was moving along the highway. As it neared closer, he could see that it was a massive articulated truck loaded up with timber.

He waved his arms and thumbed for a lift, but the driver didn't slow and it sailed past them towards the bend.

"Want me to try next time?"

Shaun shook his head, but deep down he suspected she'd have more luck. Who'd stop for a dodgy looking man coming out of the ditch?

They sat for another hour. The road was deserted. It was a Saturday, but still, they could sure do with some luck.

'What's that?... Shaun!"

The unmistakable popping of a Harley Davidson engine punctured the still air.

"Get down."

Shaun scooted under the fern hide with Claire, not daring to peek out.

The popping soon turned into a rumbling.

His ears tried to differentiate the sounds.

One, two, three bikes?

Claire had slowed them down, but they were out and about now, searching for them.

He felt Claire's heart beating fast as he held her close against his chest. The sound of the motorbikes was louder now but they'd slowed and their engines were ticking over. They'd stopped as they reached the road.

He held his breath and waited. Would they see the fern shelter across the road from them?

Then, a moment later came a roar as the bikers twisted their throttles and three big engines opened out accelerating around the bend and away.

Shaun let out a jagged breath and Claire gazed into his eyes.

"They're heading to the lodge, aren't they?"

She'd read his mind.

"Probably."

"We going there too?"

Shaun smirked.

"You ever play hide and seek as a kid?"

"Yeah. Why?"

"Did ya ever go back to where you'd looked before?"

"So we're heading to the lodge too," she said, carefully studying her swollen ankle.

"It's not too bad, but I'm definitely gonna need a ride."

"Straight up, Boss. They're pakaru. Totally munted. Gonna need some new leads from town."

"Bugger!"

Cobra King studied the motorcycles coolly. So simple. And everyone one of them so far as he could tell had been rendered useless. Never mind this Irish dude's beef, Sion Edwards was starting to piss him off too.

"Ah, Boss? Come take a squizz at this."

He followed the voice back into the front room. On the laptop, the camera they'd recently installed on the front of the property had picked up a shadow. The recording showed that it was definitely the girl. She was the one who'd sabotaged the bikes.

The younger biker chuckled as he watched her in action.

"She's as mean as, that one."

King raised an eyebrow too. He liked this girl. She sure had some balls to not shoot through. To come back and do that. The scar he'd seen on her neck was no accident. This one was a warrior. And with Māori blood, no question about that.

"She from town?"

Nik, his right-hand man pulled a face.

"Not whanau, that's for sure."

"She been hangin' around Dargarei? Find out who she is, yeah? Make some calls."

His thoughts were disrupted by a mobile phone ringing out.

He gave Nik a look, and taking the hint his young, trusted henchman took the phone out of the room to answer the call.

Five minutes later, he came back in. Like his boss, Nik wore a swirling tribal tattoo across his face and neck.

"Flight come in on time?" King asked.

"He'll be in Dargarei this arvo."

"Did ya stall him till tomorrow without it looking too suss?"

"Yeah. He's psyched though, I can tell. Asked me about the meat plant again."

"What did ya say?"

"Told him to rack off. That we'd let him put a bullet in their skulls and that was it."

King nodded contemplatively.

"He'll wait. And he's not to touch the girl."

They couldn't have gone far, but the longer time went on the less chance they had of finding them.

"The boys check the compound again?"

"Ah yeah. They're on it King, but they're sure to be gone by now. They could be lost in the forest, but? Up one of them false tracks, eh?"

King agreed.

"They'll be trying to head back to the lake for their gear and some wheels to get outta here."

"Hey, boss?"

An older biker, bald with a long beard came rushing in, stumbling a little uncertainly as King stared at him meanly for intruding.

"Uhh, sorry to break in, King. The Harleys at the back. She missed 'em."

CHAPTER 20

--------- ✳ ---------

Three more trucks and one ute have passed without stopping.

I can feel my ankle swelling up but I keep schtum about it. It's not too bad, only a twist. Anyway, we've enough to think about without Shaun worrying about that.

"My turn."

"No way."

His voice is full of concern.

"What if the gang come back up the road? You can't move fast enough on that ankle."

"Watch me."

I pull myself up from the hide and smoothing out my jeans and t-shirt, I stand waiting for a lift.

Time is ticking by. It's well after midday and the early summer sun is scorching. A milk tanker gives me hope when it slows down, but it carries on around the bend in front of us.

Another one, this time a delivery van. I smile sweetly and stick out my thumb, but no joy either.

My stomach's growling and my throat's parched but the only thing we can do is wait. And hide if we hear the bikes.

"What's that?"

Shaun lifts the binoculars to his eyes but I can see it clearly. It's an old hatchback car.

"I've got a good feeling about this one," I tell him, willing it to come true.

"How about we try together?"

"Alright."

Shaun puts the rucksack onto his back and I smooth down my hair.

As the car approaches, we stick out our thumbs and I take the weight off my bad ankle. It's throbbing but I've no time to feel sorry for myself.

Shaun shoots me a grin.

"It's slowing down."

I hold onto his shoulder and hobble with him towards the hatchback that has stopped in front of us.

"You two alright there?"

An elderly gentleman in a checked shirt and jeans that come halfway up his middle is at the wheel.

"Yeah, we've been for a hike but my girlfriend's sprained her ankle. Don't s'pose we could hitch a lift with ya?"

"Trampin' eh? Yeah, no worries. Hop in."

I try to hide the relief flooding through me and send up a silent prayer. *Thank you.*

"I'm Joe."

We introduce ourselves quickly.

"Brits, eh? On ya hols?"

"No, we've moved out here."

"Ah yeah. Wanna ride into town?"

"We're living out at the lake. Can ya drop us by the road off to it?"

"And have you limping back? No bloody way. I'll take you."

"You sure?"

"Yeah. Good as gold."

From the back seat, I give Shaun an anxious nudge with my good foot into the back of his seat. I don't want this nice old chap getting caught up in anything.

"We wouldn't wanna be puttin' you out, Joe."

"Hey! It's what we do around here. 'Sides which, if you're stayin' at Jake's Place, I reckon we're neighbours. I've got the section of land next to yours."

I lean back. There's nothing more to be said about it.

"Uh, Claire?"

Shaun leans over at me hastily and ducks his head down passing me the rucksack onto the back well of the car.

"Check in my bag for my inhaler, will ya?"

I stretch down to it at the precise moment three Harley Davidson's scream past us. We're both bent over. It's unlikely we've been seen.

Shit! That was close.

I pull out a few bits and pieces in the rucksack and look longingly at the muesli bar I've discovered.

"Sorry, Shaun, you must have left it at the lodge."

"You alright, son?"

"Yeah,"

He turns back around and leans back into the front seat, faking it, focusing on his breaths.

"It's the dust on the roads," I bullshit, "Makes him wheezy sometimes."

The old farmer looks at him, worried.

"I'll turn down the air."

"Thanks, Joe. He'll be alright. He's been doing this breathing technique. It helps him get through it most of the time."

Shaun recovers miraculously after a couple of minutes and I can see the lake as we take the bend. We're nearly at the lodge.

"We'll be good from here. Save your car."

"You sure?"

"Yeah, my ankle's fine now," I lie.

"Well, alright."

He pulls up at the main beach area alongside another van. The hot weather's drawn a few families here today.

"Can I take your phone number?" I ask gratefully. "Get you over for something to eat one evening."

"Thank you," he twinkles. "I look forward to it,"

"Us too."

Shaun shakes his hand.

"You've been a lifesaver, Joe."

He will never know how true that is.

I get out of the car, trying my best to hide the pain as I put my ankle to the floor and wave him cheerfully away.

We perch ourselves on a picnic bench next to a family enjoying a picnic.

Seeing me eyeing up the chicken legs on the next table Shaun hands me the muesli bar from the rucksack.

"Gee, thanks."

I split it with him.

"What next?"

The two Poms weren't at the lodge.

Cobra King's boys had taken hours. Precious time had been ticking away. What with getting new spark-plug leads in town and then hangin' around the lake on the way back watching out for them.

"What about the dead-end tracks? Did someone check them out?"

Nik glanced shiftily at an older biker standing by the quad bike, his inked arms folded defensively.

"All the blind cut-offs had been already marked out."

"What the..?"

Nik nodded back at the biker and they all waited apprehensively for King to speak.

"Get the boy here. Now."

"*Aw, King...*"

The boss gave the older biker, Rawiri's father, a withering look.

"Leave it, cus," the guy next to him mumbled.

The father hung his head and spat.

"I'll go get him."

Rawiri was over by the dogs mending the broken shed.

He'd seen the men coming and going all morning. Keeping out of the way, making yourself busy was harder than it looked.

"Boss wants to see ya, son."

The look in his dad's eyes confirmed he was in deep shit.

Eleven and a half thousand miles, two days solid stuck in a seat in the air to be told on arrival that Sion Edwards and Claire Williams had slipped through the net.

Irish slammed his boot hard into the flimsy side table, sending the tea and coffee tray flying across his Dargarei motel room.

Bollocks!

Slamming the door behind him Irish left the motel and started marching into town, trying to manage the rage welling up inside of him. They couldn't be far. A couple of Brits fresh off the plane. They must stand out like sore thumbs in a place like this. Like him.

He paced angrily along the bank of the muddy river, following it towards the centre of town. He had to get on top of the problem. Find out more. If these bloody amateurs couldn't do, he'd have a pop at them himself. Do the job and then go home. Easy peasy. Calmer now and with the kernel of a plan, Irish walked along the main street of this Hicksville town.

Something about Dargarei reminded him of back home. Not now, but back in the day, before the malls and the internet. It had the kind of locally owned stores where everyone knew you, like The Beatles wrote about in Penny Lane.

He strolled into a large cafe bar halfway along the street. Its name, big and bright on the front hoardings gave him the impression that this was the main joint in town. And there were a fair few punters in there from what he could see from the outside. Surely, Sion or Claire had found their way in here?

He ordered an Americano at the counter, spying as he did so the whisky bottle on the top shelf.

"And a double shot of that Red Label," he said pointing to it.

The whisky was Scottish but it'd do.

The long-haired woman with a big green necklace behind the counter raised an eyebrow.

"Tough day, huh?"

She passed him first the coffee, then the double generously poured out without a measure.

"Yeah, summat like that."

"You're not from around these parts, eh?"

He instinctively clammed up and then checked himself, forcing a smile.

"I'm looking for a Claire Williams. She's a friend of mine. Don't happen to know her, do ya? Or where she's stayin'?"

"Yeah, hun, just happens I do."

The attractive woman beamed back at him and then pointed to a row of canvas photographs on the wall.

"She lives there."

Irish studied the row of canvas photographs on the wall. They were the same shot taken at different times of the day and mounted in sequence, moving from the pink light of misty dawn through to a golden sunset out over the water. The girl had talent. Pity that those photos would be her last.

"That's some place."

"Claire did those. Haven't told her yet. The canvases came yesterday and they all sold in less than an hour. I've kept them up until she can order more and I've sold ten more of the early morning one."

"Can you give me directions?"

She scrawled a basic route for him onto a paper napkin and he pocketed it in his jeans.

"And you are?"

"Irish."

"Is that even a name?"

His icy stare sent a shiver running through her.

"So, how exactly d'ya know Claire, again?" she uttered a little shakily.

Knocking back the whisky in a single swallow Irish left the coffee untouched and handed her a fifty.

"Keep the change, love."

On his way out of the door he tried not to stare at the tough young man with a fully tattooed face striding past him into the cafe.

"Nik."

Tia smiled uneasily as she turned back from the till and saw her cousin coming through the door.

He sat down on a stool at the counter, sweeping away the full coffee cup and the empty glass in front of him.

Tia began hastily clearing the cup and glass. Nik stretched his hand out, covering her arm and clamping it fast against the countertop.

"So... Claire Williams?" he said, his eyes boring into hers. "Heard that she's a mate of yours?"

"Uh ...Yeah, Nah, Nik ...Why you askin'? What's it to you? The pale fulla you passed at the door was askin' the same thing?"

"He was?"

"Yeah. Called himself Irish."

Nik spun around, even though he knew the guy was long gone.

"Nik? Cus?"

He turned back and she met her cousin's eye, holding his gaze.

"You gotta minute?"

Nik nodded.

"Not here. Upstairs. We need to talk."

CHAPTER 21

--------*---------

"Wait here and keep watch."

Shaun kisses me lightly on the lips then dashes from the bushes where we're hiding, across the track and up towards the lodge and the barn.

Three bikes came past us when we were on the road to the lake, but Shaun needs to be sure that they've not left one of their biker goons as a watchman.

Ten minutes later he's back.

"I think they're gone but for now, we're best hiding in the barn."

"The barn?"

"You'll see."

I hold onto his shoulder and we move cautiously across the yard.

On seeing me, the hens scratching in the coop start to squawk, totally giving away our position.

"Traitors," I hiss at them as we pass.

He shakes his head.

"In all my special forces missions, I've never been sold out by a bunch of hens."

Inside the barn he leads me through to the second chamber in the shed and gets the ladder out, leaning it carefully against a beam.

"Is your ankle alright to climb up?"

"Yes."

I carefully step up the rungs, intrigued.

"Woah! It's a good job I didn't know about this."

At the top of the ladder is a concealed loft space kitted out with camping basics. A mattress and pillows, a blanket, a lamp, a basic stove.

"Why?"

"Celia told me off for accepting the job over the internet without doing checks on you first. She said how did I know that you weren't some weirdo who locks up women in basements. Or sells them to the Asian sex market, whatever that is."

"She said that about me?"

His bright blue eyes widen.

"Not exactly. She told me you were a real nice bloke."

"Oh she did, did she?"

He flashes me a flirty smile.

"And let's not forget, you're also completely gay."

"And if you'd have seen this place after she'd said all of that?"

"I'd've run a mile."

"I'm glad you didn't. This lodge was used by the Brits for witness protection. So it makes sense that it's got a hideout," he explains, pulling the ladders up after him.

"It's the best shot we've got for now."

I sit down on the mattress and hesitantly take off my trainer to examine my ankle. The bruising is coming out and it's swollen up.

"Here, let me see," he says, easing over beside me.

"It's a twist that's all."

Taking my ankle gently in his hands he checks it over too.

"Best you keep it raised. Lie down flat," he says pushing me back lightly onto the mattress.

He takes the rucksack and puts it under my foot.

"I'll go over to the house and get some ice for it."

He hovers over me for a second, gazing down at me.

I've waited so long for this man, the last thing I want to do now is to lie injured with a bag of peas on my ankle.

Stretching my arms up around his neck, I draw him down towards me.

"The ice can wait. But I can't."

I've lit the fuse.

Heat floods my core as his strong hands lift me back up onto him and he takes me in his arms.

Our lips crash together, his hand cradling my head as our tongues greedily duel. His fingers feverishly bunch my hair as my mouth begins to trail kisses along his jaw.

"Oh God, Claire. I've wanted you for so long."

Bolts of electricity fire through me as I feel the power of his desire building up inside him and his hardness rubbing against me as his hand pulls me even closer onto him, lingering under the curve of my ass.

I quickly free him of his t-shirt. Then mine's thrown off too. Soon most of our clothes lie in a heap beside us as we strip each other in a frenzy of pent-up passion and desire.

"*Ahh!*"

It escapes from deep within him as my breasts brush up against his chest, my nipples pebbling at the touch of him. I've waited too long to feel this too. Skin on skin. His warm body up close next to mine.

"I was gonna be wearing something fancy. Satin and lace."

"I saw them," he whispers into my ear, moving us back down to the mattress. "I love the purple ones."

His mouth along my neck makes me shiver, and flames of longing and need lick through me as his fingers fervently feel their way, paying zealous attention to my breasts.

Then, his lips are on them. He teases first one then the other nipple, sucking and nipping in pain and pleasure, driving me even crazier for him as his lips travel southwards.

He makes short work of my plain black panties, casting them away. My breathing quickens and soon I'm lost to him. My mind is mangled as he claims all of me with his mouth until finally, I'm on the edge. And he senses it too. He pulls away and watches me, seeing my whole body trembling for him to finish what he's started. It's delicious torture that makes me even more desperate for his touch.

"Shaun!"

I'm not too proud to beg.

"You're so beautiful," he murmurs and then I fall apart as he takes me one more time.

And then it's my turn to discover him completely too. Exploring the ridges of his muscular body; his sculpted chest, his abs, tasting all of him. Massaging him gently with my fingers and my mouth, I work my own brand of torturous teasing, bringing him to the brink too.

"Claire. Stop."

He lets out a shaky breath.

"I want you so badly, but I don't have any..."

"*Shh* ...it's okay."

We'll talk later about all of that. He's a keeper and I want him so much too, I can hardly breathe. I can tell by the desire in his eyes that he can't help himself any longer either.

Flipping me onto my back, he covers me with his body. And then, it's me kissing him. And there's no more talking to be done as I wind my legs around him, feeling his shivers of anticipation. I'm not letting go. My eyes gaze into his and I urge him on, savouring the moment as he fills me.

"*Ahh!* Claire."

Then, moving together as one he takes me with him, slowly, gently at first. Then harder and faster. Sweeping me away with him on an insistent ebbing and flowing tide, rocking me back to a deep primal place where I can no longer help myself. And where I find myself crying out his name, tensing tight and letting go. He joins me there too, finally drowning with me under the crashing waves.

"Can I help you?"

Frank Plunkett wandered over to the pale-skinned man eyeing

up the hunting knives in the cabinet by the counter in his camping store.

"Can I see that one?"

The dark-haired stranger pointed at the seventeen-inch razor-sharp bowie knife.

"Err... Sir? May I suggest this one?"

Frank unlocked the cabinet drawer and pulled out one of the more modest blades to the right.

"Stainless steel, gripped handle to prevent slipping. It's probably a more practical option for your needs up here. Guttin' fish and stuff."

The freckled man gave him a cool stare.

"How do you know what my needs are?"

Frank nodded.

The stranger spoke like one of The Beatles, but there was none of that famous cheeky humour in the accent of this Liverpudlian. This man was all business.

"Yes, S'pose you're right," Frank conceded and returned the smaller knife into the cabinet. Reluctantly, he extracted the bowie knife and placed it on the counter.

Irish picked it up and ran the long blade along his other hand meditatively. It wasn't a razor, but it would do.

"And do you stock guns here too?"

"Got a gun room out back," Frank said cautiously. "For customers with a firearms licence."

"Of course."

Irish put the knife back onto the counter's glass top and turned his attention to other items in the store.

Browsing, he cast his eye over a hat and then his eyes fell on an expensive backpack balancing up on a high hook above him to the right of the counter.

"Here, let me help you with that."

He stepped back to allow Frank past to stretch up high for the large travel bag.

In one sharp move, snatching the bowie knife off the counter-top, Irish launched himself onto Frank from behind. Riding his back to overpower him, he pulled him down to the ground.

Then, with Frank face down, prostrate to the floor, he strad-dled him, his knees pressing into Frank's arms, pinning them down on the ground to the sides.

He pulled Frank's head back expertly and held the razor-sharp blade to his throat as if he was about to give Frank as a sacrificial offering to the gods.

"Gunroom. The keys. Now."

"They're in my pocket."

With the knife held firmly to his neck from behind, he moved himself free of Frank's pinned down torso. Then slowly he pulled Frank up from the floor.

"Which pocket?"

"The left."

"Gimme them. You try anything and I'll slit yer throat."

And he would too, Frank had no doubt about that. But, there was no way he would roll over and take this either if he had half a chance.

Reaching slowly for his pocket, Frank reluctantly pulled out the set of keys.

Irish snatched them from him, looking twitchily around him and until finally he clapped eyes on some Gorilla tape over on a stand to the side.

"You and me. We're gonna take a little walk over there."

With the blade close to his artery, Frank did as he was told.

"Now, get down on the floor!"

Frank went to kneel, but as he did so, he saw his opportunity. In one desperate lunge, he flung himself back onto Irish.

"Gimme the knife you little…"

The slick blade sank into Frank's soft abdomen like a skewered marshmallow. The blood came after. It took a moment or two, but when it came it flowed in an incessant, gushing stream from the large hole in his abdomen.

Frank looked down at it in horror.

Futilely, he tried to stick his fingers in to stem the bleeding. He had to stay still. Try to patch it up. Hope that he wouldn't lose too much blood. Pray that help and an ambulance would get there soon.

"If you'd have done what I said."

He callously wiped the bloody blade clean on the shoulder of Frank's checked shirt.

"I'll give yer one more chance 'cos I like ya. You've got balls,"

Irish grazed the tip of the blade across Frank's neck. Moving it up, the tip scratched along his cheek.

"Tell yer what? You show me which is the key for the gun room and I promise not to cut off your ears."

CHAPTER 22

---------✳---------

"So what do we do next?" I whisper into Shaun's impressively sculpted chest as we lie together on the mattress.

He bends his neck forward and whispers in my ear. His suggestions make me laugh out loud.

"Already?"

Apparently so.

And we make love again. Slowly and sensually. Lazily, like we have all the time in the world, which I know we don't.

But, oh my. *This man!* My legs are numb, my head's fried and my heart's full to bursting. And all I want to do now is to curl up in his arms and sleep, right here in the rafters of the barn.

But we can't.

We lie quietly together, my head on his chest, our bodies still slick with sweat.

"Seriously Shaun, what are we gonna do?"

"We could run?" he suggests a little half-heartedly. "Take the car and get far away from here?"

"Is that what you want?" I ask, propping myself up on my elbow so I can see his face.

He brushes his hand tenderly along my cheek.

"We should call the police. They already know about the Cobras."

My eyes meet his.

"If it's not the Cobras, then will it be some other gang? Are we gonna spend the rest of our lives running?"

He's quiet for a while. Chewing it over. Then he presses his lips onto mine.

"We better get dressed."

He sits up.

"Where we going?"

"To the house. Get a shower. Something to eat. Find that sexy underwear of yours."

He blows kisses on my belly making me squeal.

"We're staying put at the lodge. Facing this out."

"And what about the Cobras?"

"We'll keep watch. If we see them heading our way, we'll hide back here."

After Nik had gone, Tia left the café too, crossing over the road from the café to the florist shop. June usually never missed a trick, but she was staring back blankly at Tia now.

"A Brit you say?"

"Yeah. With an accent like from that soap you always watch?"

"What, Coro?"

"Ah yeah! That one. Coronation Street."

"No, sorry, babes. Not seen any Poms around here today."

"He's about this high?" Tia persisted, "Dark hair, pale skin, freckles?"

"Ah! You mean the guy who went into the camping shop about half an hour ago?"

"Choice!"

Tia smiled back at her, already running.

"June, I owe ya."

She'd had a terrible feeling about this *Irish* since he left. The bloke was a weirdo and she needed to throw him off the scent. Get that napkin with the directions to the lake back off him. Call Claire?

By the camping store, she reached in her bag for the phone, her finger hovering over Claire's number.

After she'd told Nik everything he'd made some calls too. Then he'd left her to meet up with King. Nik was a brave one. Some-one had to tell King and it may as well be him. He was like a son to the big guy. Nik had agreed with her. Once King knew about Claire, he'd be there like a shot.

She shook her head and put the phone back into her bag. She really liked that girl but Nik had told her to keep out of it, he'd handle it. Nik was family, but even so, it was best not to mess with Cobra business or with King.

She turned to go into the camping store. Something told her to check in on Frank anyway. She was curious to see what that Brit had bought.

"Frank? You there?"

Tia called out again as she wandered into the shop.

"You seen a man with pale skin and freckles? Funny accent? ... Frank?"

A small gurgling sound was all he could manage. But it was enough. That, and the pool of blood that swept in a thick red carpet that Tia followed to where he lay.

He'd been trying to reach the phone but he was too weak.

"*Struth!* Frank. Don't move. I'm calling 111."

She made the call and then went back over to him, trying to stem the bleeding too by pressing onto the wound in his stom-ach, willing the ambulance to get there as soon as.

From the gun room at the back Irish heard voices drifting from the shop. A woman calling out. She sounded hysterical. But he wasn't fussed about that. He'd got what he needed.

Coolly pocketing an extra box of ammo, he stored the two pump-action shotguns in a camouflage-coloured gun bag. Farmer guns. Still, at the end of the day, all he needed was two shots to hit the target and he'd achieve what he'd come all this way to do.

It's so good to be clean again. And to be here, in this lovely house with Shaun.

He joins me in the lodge kitchen and sits on a stool at the island where I'm chopping up vegetables. I'm trying to make us some dinner with one eye still watching the track through the window.

"You've done a great job with those rooms."

"Thanks. They're ready for guests."

"Let's wait till next season. I kinda want it to be you and me for a while."

I don't disagree with that idea. I want us to spend time alone together too.

"These are amazing, Claire."

He points towards the opened parcel.

I've seen them too. They're not bad. I'm going to put them in the guest rooms.

"You need to do this professionally."

"Funny, you say that. Tia thinks so too. I ordered her a set of the lake and she's put them up for sale in the café in town. She was trying to be nice to me but I don't think they'll sell. Anyone can take a photo."

"But not like these. I'd buy them. They're stunning."

He goes to the window and takes a good look around. The place is deserted from what I can see, but he goes out to re-check the barn anyway and then drops down to the shoreline from where he can see the whole of the picnic area across the lake.

"One car left, hikers by the looks of it. All the other day-trippers have gone. I've left the barn door open and the ladder ready, in case we need to bolt."

A shiver runs down my spine.

"I was going to ask you," I say, chopping up a pepper and trying hard to jump back into our happily-ever-after dream. "What d'you think about turning the barn into a bunkhouse?"

It takes him a minute and then his face cracks into a broad, beaming smile.

"We could do like an outdoor pursuits centre. Kayaking, fishing, climbing, bushcraft, that sort of thing. It'd be awesome."

I smirk.

"You'll have to get someone in to teach fishing."

He nips my waist at that, making me shriek.

"Instead of clearing the land to farm," he carries on, "We could build eco-lodges, tree houses, do glamping pods and camping out in the bush? What d'you think, Claire? You and me? Together?"

"Is that a job offer?"

He takes the knife carefully from me and holds both of my hands, interlacing my fingers in his. My heart is pumping as he holds my gaze, searching into my eyes like he's exploring my soul.

Then, I can't believe it. *Holy Shit!* He's dropping down onto one knee.

"Marry me, Claire? Let me spend the rest of my life with you."

I'm stunned. One minute I'm chopping a pepper, the next I'm getting married. Getting married. To Shaun.

"Yes!"

My hand's covering my mouth in shock.

"Yes… *Yes*."

I pull him up to me and we kiss passionately. The food is forgotten as he takes me hard and fast on the granite kitchen top.

Now I've found Shaun, I'm never letting him go.

"Who was that?"

I ask afterwards, seeing him ending a call as I come back down from the bathroom.

I'm determined to restart making this meal. My stomach's growling. Abduction, escape, sex, marriage proposals; nothing is going to stop me this time from eating that pepper.

"I tried Frank. Thought I'd better warn the neighbours about the Cobras. But there was no answer. And I phoned Ari."

"What did Ari say?"

"He says to tell you congrats and that he's coming over."

"What, now? Is it safe? He's got a baby."

"Claire, honey, we gotta sort this out if we wanna stay here."

"What about the police?"

"Not yet. Ari thinks he can help us."

King listened carefully to everything Nic said.

Then he called Nic's cousin, Tia, and she confirmed it. Told him too about Frank Plunkett. Decent bloke. Nearly carked it, she said. By all accounts, it was still touch and go.

He didn't owe Frank anything. It wasn't his business. But Tia had confirmed it was this 'Irish' dude that had stabbed him.

King considered it some more. He'd brought trouble to the town. And the police would be on his back about it. They'd always lived with each other by the set of three unwritten rules:

Keep your head down.

Don't rock the boat.

Don't take the piss.

And today he'd done all three.

The sand was cooling on the west coast beach, and in the mellow afternoon light small crabs had started scuttling along the shoreline. Hundreds of them. The beach, only accessible through the dense forest, was deserted. A rare wilderness. A sacred place for his iwi, his tribe. Everything he was now, was because of them. His ancestors.

And yet, up until an hour ago, he'd had no family to call his own. None that would talk to him anymore.

They'd shunned him after his brother deserted the Cobras and set his family against him. As far as his father was concerned he'd brought shame on the family. And words like that couldn't be unsaid.

And then today, his brother had called him. Out of the blue, after fifteen long years. He'd got his number through the kid, Rawiri. And when they spoke it was like everything was all okay again.

From the call, he was right. Rawiri had split loyalties. He'd fair grilled the lad after they'd found the false trails had all been marked out, but Rawiri had toughed it out. He'd been too soft on the boy. But then, Rawiri's old man had saved his skin a few times against the Mongrel Mob and he owed him. That favour had been repaid today.

King reached behind his neck and took off his pounamu necklace. The large, spiral-twisted jadestone felt warm in his hand.

His grandmother had given it to him a long time ago, the night before he'd first gone overseas. It had comforted him in his first lonely weeks in that strange cold place on the other side of the world. It had helped him until he'd gotten on his feet, become one of the rugby boys.

And when the injury put paid to his professional rugby career and he'd found himself back in Auckland, skint, he'd nearly sold it. His gammy leg meant he couldn't do much hard graft.

He hadn't. Instead, he'd been stoked when he saw how much he could earn by selling a few wraps of the homemade skunk brought from back home. Soon he had a string of customers, a dedicated phone line and a gang of boys willing to grab some action too. And his little brother had come in on it.

When he started ruffling feathers, earning too much dosh, the Mongrels moved in to shut him down. His brother witnessed the shots; his first kill.

By rights, he should be facing the rest of his days in prison. But instead of setting himself up against him in court, his brother had cleaned himself up, then gone back north and set his family against him.

All things considered, he'd have far preferred to have taken the jail time.

King rolled the jade twists in the palm of his large hand. It felt comforting now too. So many things to consider.

Was what Tia had said to him, right? The facts didn't all fit.

He owed Irish no loyalty. When the cops linked him to the Cobras, there'd be a raid and the whole outfit'd be smashed up. Finished. He figured they had a week to clear out and move on.

But he still had a choice. His brother had made that clear in the phone call. He'd opened the door for him. To come back to his family again.

But was he ready to step back in?

CHAPTER 23

---------✷---------

The plan was simple, Irish considered as he waited in the beach car park by the lake.

The late afternoon sunshine glistening on the still waters, lapping onto the white sandy shoreline. Another time, he'd like to take a holiday, see a bit more of this country.

This place was far too good for the likes of double-crossing government agents. Cops were bad enough, but guys like Sion Edwards who went undercover, they were on another level. And he was going to pay for what he'd done. To his friends, his brother, to him.

Forget the jokers who'd brought him here. It'd taken him ten seconds, if that, to get directions and find the pair. Cobras, he snorted derisively. More like slow worms. If that lot of jokers were thrown out of a plane, they'd struggle to find the ground.

He'd spied the cops swarming around the camping store as he drove past, slowly along the main street on his way out to the lake. He'd squeezed the car through, past the parking spaces stacked up with ambulances and police cars.

He didn't have long before they'd be tracking him down. He'd cleared out of that crumby motel and had even managed to book himself onto a flight the next evening. He eyed up the gun bag in the seat well beside him. His ducks were lined up. All he needed to do now was finish the job.

He'd seen the outline of Edwards a few minutes before. But, this ex-soldier was no pushover. He needed the element of surprise. So, later, when the lights came on in the house and the love birds were settling down, maybe enjoying a glass or two of wine and relaxing, he'd go in there. Sneak in silently, creep up to the living room, kitchen, bedroom, wherever they were and... Bang. Bang. Happy days.

He still had the knife. He'd had his first taste of Kiwi blood. If he had half a chance, he'd tie them up. Play a little before he shot them. Indulge in a little slicing. Listen to their screams as he mutilated them. Piece by piece.

◆ ◆ ◆

"Mate!"

Ari stepped out of the rusting saloon car he'd borrowed for the trip and embraced his friend by the steps of the porch.

"Wow, this place is amazing," Ari said, checking out the lodge and then the view of the lake.

"I said I'd get you over here," Shaun joked grimly. "Thanks for coming."

"No worries. Is Claire here?"

Shaun looked at him, puzzled, then nodded.

"Cool."

Ari got out his phone and walked towards the water to make the short call.

"What's going on, bro?"

In the distance, Shaun heard the popping noise he'd been dreading.

He spun on his heels to see where Claire was.

"What you doin' Ari?...Mate!... What the..?... You selling us out?"

Ari laid his large hand on Shaun's shoulder.

"Chill, bro. It's sweet."

"What d'ya mean?"

Claire rushed out onto the porch and watched fearfully too as the motorbikes were getting closer, their rumbling becoming ever more thunderous. They were still out of view but in the distance, a thick cloud of dust rose from the track. There were far more than three this time.

"Shaun, trust me, bro."

Shaun didn't know what to think. Was Ari in on this too? He'd sent Rawiri. Had the boy saved him or had he led him to the trap with Claire as the bait?

Did Ari know about the contract on them? Was he trying to score a few bucks himself?

Shaun was torn. He looked searchingly at Claire.

Head high, strong and proud, she had a stillness about her now as she faced her fate.

"We stay," she said quietly, her eyes transfixed by the lake.

"We need to face them. Have it out."

The roar soon became deafening.

The three stood on the steps of the wrap-around decked porch watching their visitors coming closer.

And soon, twenty or more heavy-duty motorcycles were rolling towards them, ridden by a chapter of the meanest-looking men. And Shaun had seen a fair few bad-ass dudes in his time.

At the front was the toughest of them all. The Cobra King, riding his Harley Davidson like a pure-bred stallion.

They passed the parked up car by the beach and came to a halt up right in front of the lodge. The others stayed in their seats on their bikes, but their leader dismounted his stead and now squared-up in front of the three on the porch.

Like Ari, he was another mountain of a man, a modern-day warrior with his shaved head and fully tattooed face.

Shaun watched on.

The Cobra King's eyes were fixed on Claire.

In turn, she held his gaze defiantly.

"What do you want?" she uttered bravely.

"I hear you're looking for Tane Matene?"

"Yeah, what's it to you? D'you know him?"

He heard her breath catch.

She edged her way towards him, down the steps of the decking and stood before him.

"Dad?"

He cleared his throat and a couple of the men gave each other a dubious look.

For the first time in his life, King looked unsure of himself.

Uncharacteristically tentatively he took her arm and bent his face down to hers, touching their nose together.

"Claire!"

He swept her into his arms and held her tightly.

"You knew about me?"

He nodded.

"Yeah. Your mother. She wrote me."

Claire shook her head. All these years and she thought he'd never known he had a daughter.

"Tia called me. Told me you was here. And then, Ari said too… But your mum, she changed your name?"

"Yeah. I took the Williams name when she got married again. She moved on with a new family. As soon as I was sixteen, I left."

Shaun heard the pain in her voice as she spoke.

Reaching around his neck, the giant biker took off his pounamu necklace. His huge paws placed it gently around Claire's neck.

"My kuia gave me this. You've found your family now."

"Kuia?"

"My gran," he said, stroking her hair, "The double twists means two peoples joined. Sticking together, however far apart, whatever shit goes down. Our kuia was right. I found you."

Leaning up she kissed the deep blue lines of his cheek.

"Thank you."

Shaun gave Ari a puzzled look.

"Tane's my big brother."

Ari shrugged.

"Guess that makes me Claire's uncle."

"You knew that, then? The time we went climbing?"

"Yeah about that," Ari said, kicking the wooden decking boards with his foot "Me and him. It's complicated, eh."

"And that's how I got to go in the waka?"

Ari winked at him.

"And when I saw her, I knew straight away. So did Mum. We all did."

Shaun shook his head. There was a whole heap of questions to ask, a whole pile more than the answers he'd been given.

And judging by Claire's face, it was the same for her too.

"What about the contract?" Claire breathed, overcome by it all.

King jerked his head and the gang moved over, away from their bikes towards the house. Shaun tensed and stood firm, reassured only by Ari's large hand resting on his shoulder.

"The dude's in Dargarei."

"What? Irish?" Shaun asked.

The big warrior raised an eyebrow in confirmation.

"And he's done some damage. Stole himself a couple of guns and he's on his way up here."

It was the worst news.

"What kind of guns?"

"Hard to say. Frank's mainly got shotguns. Good for popping off the odd possum or wild goat."

"Frank, did ya say? As in, Camping Store Frank?"

"Yeah."

Shaun studied King's face. There was something he wasn't being told.

"Is he still alive?"

"Yeah… Last time I heard."

King focused on the decking.

"He's been airlifted to Auckland."

Shaun rubbed his face and turned to face the house for a second. No way was anyone going to see that a tear had escaped from the corner of his eye.

His friend, the first one who'd welcomed him with open arms here was fighting for his life in a trauma unit.

Celia would be beside herself. And he was to blame.

"D'you think he's already here?" Claire asked her father, scanning the horizon anxiously.

"Hard to say. But we'd better be ready."

CHAPTER 24

---------✳---------

The swarm of motorcycles thundering past his hire car woke Irish up from his deep, dreamless snooze. He watched them as they roared past the public beach area up to the big house on the lake shore.

"Fuck!"

The Cobras had got to them first. That'd mean he'd have to pay out that bunch of amateurs, after all.

They were certainly turning up mob-handed, there had to be twenty of them, at least.

He slung the gun bag over his shoulder and locked the hire car door behind him.

He could simply rock up there? Be all English about it. Ask the nice leather-clad chaps if they'd be *total* sports and let him sort out those two young scallywags himself. If they wouldn't mind *awfully* stepping aside for him … *so he could splatter their feckin' brains like burst watermelons across the decking.*

Irish shuddered.

He'd let himself get soft. He'd been relying too much on others, people like Whitey, to do his dirty work. And he couldn't deny the fact that he was enjoying himself now. That old nutter in the camping shop, it had been like the old days again. Feeling their fear, watching them fight back even when they were so obviously defeated, it always turned him on.

He followed the line of the bushes, trying to keep out of sight of the house. In the end, he found a clump of giant spiky grass that proved the perfect covering for him.

From there, he could see that ten or more bikers had quickly made themselves at home. They were sitting on the porch. Tough nuts in leathers and heavy metal band T-shirts. Biker outlaws with semi-automatics.

They were tooled up better than he was.

His eyes twitched when he saw her come out of the house. Claire Williams. She hobbled out of the door at the back towards the bikers. She had a bad ankle. That was good. Meant she couldn't run.

He blinked then, not believing his eyes. What was she doing? She was offering them bottles of beer.

She went back inside and a little while later came out again. This time with bowls of snacks.

He'd seen everything now. How had this turned from an abduction to a *goddam* party?

Something had gone down. He wasn't sure what it was, but she certainly didn't look like she was about to meet her Maker anytime soon.

"Frank's out of surgery. The police are swarming all over Dargarei looking for Irish. They've set up roadblocks on all the routes south," Shaun announces, coming off the phone.

Celia's called him back. He's not told her much about who did it. I've told him it's not his fault but he still feels terrible about Frank. I do too.

"I'll see 'em right," Tane says gruffly, studying me sheepishly.

He's so big, his thighs scrape the underneath of the kitchen table he sits in the chair.

"Yeah, you should," I add, and he raises an eyebrow at me.

I've said enough. He knows he's not innocent in this. But I don't push it.

"Why did you never try to contact me?" I ask him straight out.

It's been bugging me. And I get the feeling that Tane, I refuse to call him King, Tane appreciates directness.

"Yer mum, when she wrote me, she sent me a baby pic. I'd got injured and I was skint. I offered to send her money when I had some, but she wanted more. She wanted me to come back. Be yer dad."

"And you didn't."

It isn't a question. It's a statement of fact.

"I'm not proud of that. I was gettin' mixed up in some heavy shit back then. I sent her a cheque a while later, but it never got cashed. I took it to mean she'd moved on."

"And that was that?"

"Ah yeah, pretty much. I always wondered about you though. Always remembered your birthday. April 23rd."

I bat away the traitorous drop rolling down my face.

I sniff.

"Seems to me like you're still into some heavy shit?"

"Yeah," he chuckles. "Questionable lifestyle choices."

Ari raises an eyebrow to that and his face is serious again.

"Doesn't have to be, bro," Ari says quietly. "Mum and Dad miss you. We all do."

"I can't leave the boys."

"I'm glad I found you, Tane," I tell him.

His eyes meet mine and I find a softness in them that takes my breath away.

"Me too, baby girl."

"Tell me about her scar."

Ari and his brother moved out onto the porch with Shaun. Bottles of beer in their hands, they sat on the decking steps looking out at the lake.

Shaun stretched out his legs.

"It was them. The Scousers. Grabbed her, tried to get her to talk. Used her to get at me."

"This Irish fulla?"

"An associate of his, yeah. He'd been Claire's boss in the bar she was working in. He was trying to make a quick buck."

Even though technically the big guy had been doing the same, Shaun noticed Tane's free hand had balled into a fist.

"If I ever meet him, he's a dead man." Tane rumbled.

"He's in prison for it."

"Just as well."

Tane Matene stared out at the lake.

"And what makes you so special? To be hunted halfway across the world?"

"I'm not gonna sugar-coat it," Shaun said honestly. "I was in the special forces."

"A soldier."

"Hmm. Yeah. Then I was in the National Crime Agency. I infiltrated gangs."

"He wants you real bad."

"I killed some people. Got a lot of Irish's mates banged up, including his little brother."

King's eyes drifted towards Ari. The look he gave him was thinly disguised. And Shaun could tell that if he had done that to the Cobras, King would have gone after him too. Hunted him down. For the honour of his brother.

The big man was quiet for a good while.

"You got quite a past too," he muttered finally.

"Yes," Shaun answered, "And I'm not proud of it."

"And you about to rat us out too? Tell the cops about the operation in the forest?"

"No," Shaun answered flatly. "Your stuff. It's none of my business. It was my job before but Sion Edwards is done. Now, I'm Shaun Cobain. And it feels... better. Much better."

The gang chief sat quietly for a few more seconds.

"You startin' over again out here, then?"

"Yeah," Shaun meditated. "Thinkin' of starting an outdoor centre."

Ari chipped in, "What? For kids?"

"For everyone. But I was thinking about a kids programme too. For kids like I was."

King swigged his beer.

"What d'ya mean?"

"Kids on the street, who get mixed up in bad stuff."

"And that was you?"

"Yeah, that was me."

Tane nodded, staring at the lake.

"Army saved me," Shaun continued. "Got me fit. Taught me skills."

"For me, it was sport," King muttered half to himself.

Ari chewed it over.

"When I went back, Dad made me learn skills passed down from our tīpuna, our ancestors."

"You guys in then?" Shaun asked quietly, taking a swig.

Ari nodded.

"Straight up?"

"Yeah."

"Shaun, mate, you can't handle the jandal without me around. Yeah, man. I'm in. You say when, you say how and I'm there."

"And yer stickin' around? No bullshit?"

It was Claire's father talking now.

Shaun met him in the eye.

"Yeah. No bullshit. Like I said, I want a quiet life here… with Claire."

Tane Matene stood up, huge, towering above him.

Sensing the challenge, Shaun lifted himself onto his feet too and faced him, fearless.

At six foot, his shoulders still came to the big guy's chest. But still, he stood holding the stare. Two warriors. Face to face. Eyeball to eyeball.

"So, Sir?" Shaun said, his blue eyes fixed, refusing to blink.

"Do I have permission to marry your daughter?"

Tane froze. His ink-lined face set hard against the Pom.

But in their stare, Shaun could see something else behind those dark impenetrable eyes that were so similar to Claire's.

Moving his head forward, Tane leaned and carefully placed his nose onto Shaun's.

He took that as a yes.

The big guy turned silently from him and sat back down.

Taking his cue, Shaun grabbed more beers from the chilly bin behind them and handed them to the brothers.

Ari gave him a friendly wink.

"You know," Tane broke the silence. "Things aren't what they used to be up here, for those of us in the horticultural trade. They're using drones and all sorts of sneaky shit, these days. Taking pictures. Spraying the forest. Raiding units."

"Nowhere's safe anymore," Ari agreed. "P'raps it's time to stop, bro. Before you push yer luck too far."

Tane sat reflectively, watching the lake, drinking his beer.

"So, what do we do about this chancer, eh? I reckon my boys set up a rota. Keep you fullas safe."

Shaun swept back his sandy hair with his free hand. "Ah, I don't want to put you guys out. Irish hasn't shown up yet. He's probably seen the bikes and high-tailed it back to the airport before the cops get him for attempted murder."

"Two of my men will stay," Tane decided, "Keep watch on the house."

"You sure?"

He nodded and gave Shaun the ghost of a smile.

"It's my little girl in there."

"I'll stay the night too, if that's alright?" Ari added. "Give you a hand if there's any bother."

"You're just after a full night's kip," Shaun joked and got up to get them a bowl of crisps.

"You're gonna come home, eh?" Ari asked his brother when Shaun had disappeared into the house, "Meet Michelle and Kauri. Mum and Dad'll be stoked."

Tane nodded.

"Yeah?".

"Yeah."

He put his hand on his brother's arm.

"It'll be sweet as, I promise, bro."

Tane Matene, Cobra King, watched his future son in law handing out the stubbies and potato chips.

He called one of the guys and signalled for a gun.

"And ammo."

Another tough dude passed him a box of cartridges.

"Keep her safe, son."

He handed the 0.22 semi-auto to Shaun.

Shaun swallowed a lump in his throat.

"I will."

Irish racked his brains as he studied what was going on at the lake house.

What was happening? He didn't understand.

They were the Cobras, alright. One biker had a huge snake inked across his bare back.

He'd paid them good money. What were they playing at? They should have caught the pair and got them ready for him, as per the deal.

Instead, they were all hanging out together. Kicking back on the porch. Hanging around the kitchen. Like happy *feckin'* families.

Behind the large flax bush, he watched them closely. Claire was inside the house. Then, it was him. Sion Edwards appeared flanked by two huge Māori men, one in cargo shorts and one dressed like the toughest biker he'd ever seen. He was massive.

And what the…? Was he right in thinking that this guy's face was tattooed over? That was one mean son of a bitch.

And they were sitting on the deck now, shooting the breeze and drinking bloody beer like they were three best buddies. This was insane.

He got one of the shotguns out of the bag and loaded it with the cartridges.

Edwards and his two new buddies were talking about something big. He watched then as the big hardcase stood up and squared up at Edwards.

Was he about to smack him one?

No. Something had been settled between them.

The hackles on the back of his neck rose. Someone walked over his grave, as his nan would say. Why did he get the feeling that his fate had just been sealed?

Pointing the barrels, Irish took aim. Fitting the shotgun snugly into the crook of his shoulder, trying to find Edwards' head.

It was a proper farmer gun, alright. Fine for rabbits, vermin. Rats.

One shot.

That was all he needed. One shot to hit the spot.

Argh!

The rat's head was obscured by the giant's shoulder and he didn't have a clear shot. And with the guns they'd got, if he did have a pop the noise would give his location away immediately. With those serious semi-automatics he'd be plastered in gunshot in seconds.

He pushed his way back into the flax bush and put the gun away.

He had no other option but to wait it out.

And if the gang stayed?

He scanned the buildings. There was a big old barn over to the side of the house with the door left wide open. If the bikers were still at the house by dusk, he'd hide in the barn.

Then, first thing, he'd break into the lodge. And shoot them in their beds.

CHAPTER 25

--------*--------

Irish got to the barn no bother.

Most of the bikers had cleared out from the house. The ones left were sitting outside on the porch drinking beer, playing a game of poker. They were tooled up but not battle-ready.

The big bugger with the mask face was still there too. Was that King? If it was, he'd be getting one in the head too. For goods and services not received.

The barn was big. He wandered through to the second room, where he couldn't resist the temptation of climbing the ladder, propped up against a ceiling beam.

It was a lucky strike.

A hideout with a mattress. A blanket lay bunched up on the bed. And pillows. Had somebody or bodies been there recently? Hiding out?

Irish sat down. His shoulders slumped as he tried to relax. It'd been one hell of a day. And it wasn't over yet.

It was strange to think that his little brother would be waking up around about now. He'd be in his cell, opening the contents of the breakfast tray that they'd been given the evening before, getting ready for another day of pushing a mop and bucket around the wings.

He felt the anger rising within him as he thought about his brother. What age would Tony's kid be by the time his dad could put him to bed? He did the maths. *Christ!* Who wants a bedtime story when they're nine?

He pulled up the ladder for added security, then sat back down on the makeshift bed. He sniffed. Was it him or did it smell like sex up here?

It'd been far too long, if he was starting to imagine the smells. For the second time, he did a mental calculation. Realising that it had indeed been far too long since he'd had his leg over, he reached for his phone to distract himself.

There was a text message from Whitey,

'Got the bird in yesterday and it's been singing.'

Below it was a number.

Yes!

With Whitey's knowledge of the prison layout, they'd been able to drop the dead pigeon from a drone when the ground-work boys were on duty. The bird's leg was ringed with Tony's cell number and inside the dead pigeon there was a mobile phone and charger.

Hastily, Irish called the number, listening to it click and then finally start ringing.

"What?"

His brother sounded groggy. Like he'd woken him up.

"Tony?"

He spoke quietly into the phone.

"Yeah. Who's this?"

"Tony, it's me. Connor."

"Where you been? You missed the visit."

He smirked. Tony was probably needing more magazines.

"I'm in New Zealand."

"New Zealand? What the fook you doin' there?"

"I found him, Tony. Sion Edwards. The Welsh grass who got you put away. I'm gonna get him back for yer."

"Irish..."

There was silence at the other end. He could hear his brother breathing.

"Don't say that," his little brother mumbled.

"What, Tony?"

"Don't. Don't say it. I don't want no more blood on my hands."

"What d'ya mean?"

"Kill him if it'll make *you* feel better. But not for me, Connor. *Never* say you did it for me."

"But, Tony... I come half ways 'round the world for ya?"

"Yeah. Ya did. 'Cos yer a crazy git and you can't stand the fact that this Sion bloke got one up on yer. This was always about you. Irish, the great fuckin' gangster. But, I want nutin' to do with it. Ya hear me, Connor? Nothin'."

The phone went dead.

He rubbed his head and put the phone back in his pocket. Then, he leaned back onto the mattress.

Was he serious? How could he say that? Everything he did was for his family.

A wave swept over him. Was he tired of all of this? Or was it the jetlag? It was the jet lag, he decided. It was an assassin in its own right, sneaking up on you quietly, rendering you helpless.

Loaded gun at his side, Connor O'Dwyer curled up on the mattress that smelled of sex.

It didn't matter what his brother thought, or who he was doing this for, anymore. The fact remained that Sion Edwards had ratted him out. And for that, tomorrow they'd all die.

Fat lot of good they've been. Two of my father's biker gang henchmen are propped up on the lodge deck outside, fast asleep. I step over them to pick up a handful of empty beer bottles. So much for guard duty.

The kitchen looks like locusts have swarmed. The cupboards are bare and beer bottles, plates and greasy bowls are strewn across the granite tops. The detritus of the night before.

Tane's asleep in one of the guest rooms. Ari in another. They were both up 'til the wee hours, 'keeping watch' supposedly. Drinking whisky with Shaun, more like.

It's real early. The sun is up but the air is still a little cool and the lake is mirror-still. It's so breathtakingly beautiful out here today, I'm *so* going to get Shaun to come out with me in the canoe. I'd wake him up now but he's still in a deep sleep.

To be honest, last night I was glad of the space. A lot has gone on in the last twenty-four hours and I needed to think about all of it. I'm engaged to Shaun. I can't stop grinning from ear to ear every time I remember that. What we did. How he makes me feel.

And I've found 'Daddy.' Cobra King. Chief gang leader. Drug dealer. A man who'd abducts girls for money. A man prepared to kill. Has killed.

Tane's hardly the kind of guy you'd want your boyfriend to meet. And yet there they were, the three of them, getting on like a house on fire.

It's a lot to get my head around. I crumb up the crusts of a stale loaf of bread and slip on my sandals by the door. What with everything going on last night, we forgot to feed the chooks.

Is Tane Matene the kind of daddy I want in my life?

And do I get to choose?

Irish was woken up by his mobile vibrating against his hip.

It was light but it felt early.

Disoriented, he took a second to remember where he was. In the barn. Waiting. *Shit!* He'd slept for too long.

And he'd missed the call.

He pressed reply. It was Pete.

"Connor? Thank God!"

"What? Why are you calling my mobile? It's not secure."

"It's too late for that. They've raided the stores."

He felt his blood draining from his face as Pete continued. Millions of pounds worth of top-grade cocaine. Seized.

"Fuck!"

"Exactly. And three of our offshore accounts have been frozen. I can't work out how they've found them."

"So, what do we do?" Irish asked, trying to recover his composure.

"I won't ask what's possessed you to take off to New Zealand but I need your arse back here, right now. If you don't, you're not gonna have a business to come back to. Everything on the ground needs to be cleaned up and closed down. They'll follow the supply chain and it's only you with the links to the dealers."

"Alright. Don't panic. I've a little business to attend to but I'm booked onto the evening flight outta here. And I can make some calls."

Irish picked up the shotgun beside him and made for the ladder, leaving the long bowie knife by the mattress.

There was no time for slicing. He needed to end this now.

Shaun woke with a start from his deep sleep.

The scream was deafening.

Claire?

His hands frantically felt the coldness of the space in the bed beside him. She'd been up for a while. And that scream was definitely hers.

Bounding from the bed, he jumped into his shorts and grabbed the loaded rifle by the bed.

Where was she?

He knew it had been too easy. They'd been caught off guard.

"Claire?"

"Boss?" The call came through the house from one of the men at the bottom of the stairs. Tane and a sleepy Ari appeared on the upstairs landing a few seconds later.

"What's going on?" Ari asked.

A gruff voice from below.

"He's got a gun to her head."

"Where is he?"

"Out front."

"Sion Edwards?" The loud shout came from outside.

There was no mistaking the scouse accent. It was Irish. And he sounded pumped up. Volatile. Shaun's stomach lurched. In his professional opinion, he sounded liable to shoot her.

"Get here," he screamed towards the house again. "Or I'll blow her fuckin' brains out, you hear me?"

King stared at Shaun.

"What you gonna do?"

Shaun chewed his lip. The gang leader was asking him?

"Gimme a second. Let me take a look."

Nearing his bedroom window, he moved the shutter so he could stay out of view.

The bastard. He'd got Claire kneeling on the lake shoreline with two barrels pointed into the base of her skull. An instant kill.

His heart melted. She was shaking and making small whimpering sounds, trying to keep it together. But she was terrified. *Claire!*

He went back to the landing. He needed to think straight.

"I've got a clear shot but it's too risky. If he touches the trigger, she's dead."

"Call the police?" Ari suggested.

"Yeah... But, what about in the meantime?" Shaun replied, "The guy's about to pop."

His eyes met Tane's.

They both knew the only thing left to do. But who would go?

"Can you cover me?" Shaun asked him, holding out the rifle towards Tane.

A big hand covered his, holding it and the rifle firm in the space between them.

"You're the snipper," Tane's voice rumbled. "You need to do your job. Save us both."

Shaun put his free hand on the big man's shoulder. Tane was

right.

Shaun nodded at Tane.

"Be careful."

Slipping on a black t-shirt and baseball cap, he edged back to the window and got into position in the shadow of the shutter with his loaded gun.

Above Irish's head, the bedroom window slowly opened, little-by-little, inch-by-inch. Wide enough to reveal the black barrel of his rifle.

Shaun's eye drilled down the scope, focussing on the Scouser's head, consciously, desperately trying to block all his fears for Claire from his mind.

If he was going to do this, he needed to be the sniper again. No matter how much he wanted to rage, to blow the guy's head off. He needed to shut all of that out.

Slow down his pulse and breathe... In... Then out... In... Then out... Line him up... And wait... Wait for that one moment, the sweet spot, when he was in the cross-hairs... and she was safely away.

"*Irish!*"

The thunderous bellow rolled from the lounge windows as Tane Matene, Cobra King, burst out onto the decking. Shoulders broad, head high.

Irish shot agitated glances between the girl and the huge beast of a man squaring up to him.

"What the f..?"

His voice trailed as he finally took in the size and spectacle before him.

A warrior, towering tall, arms folded in a warlike stance. Behind him, two built giants pointed their rifles his way.

"Let her go."

Tane Matene took a defiant and deliberate step towards Claire.

The Adam's apple on Irish's skinny neck bobbed. What was he going to do? Shoot her and get killed himself? Or hold out for Edwards? Use his brains, try a negotiation?

"King?"

Shaun heard the Liverpudlian's voice cracking. His finger was poised. The sight was lined up solidly in place. But the Scouser's gun stayed jammed resolutely to Claire's head.

No shot.

Another giant step. The gang leader's shadow stretched forward. It was now touching Claire's knees.

She looked up shakily towards her father.

Irish twitched.

"We had a deal, King. *A feckin' deal.* She's mine. And so is Sion Edwards."

"Let my girl go."

"Your girl?" Irish asked edgily.

Another step. Tane was ground level, five feet away from him.

"Stay where you are, or I'll do her, *right now.*"

The gun wavered for a second away from Claire towards her father.

Shaun's finger poised, ready to squeeze.

Too late. The gun swung back to the base of her head.

Dammit! No shot.

"Let her go!"

The bellowed order rolled around the wind and the shoreline in the stillness.

From the bedroom window, through the scope, Irish's body shifted a little to the left. He was wobbling. He was gone.

Shaun got ready again.

"Give me Sion Edwards."

Irish's voice sounded reedy and dry.

Tane stood tall and Shaun waited for the next move.

Would the warrior come and drag him down there? Swap him for his daughter?

He was prepared to go.

But Tane stood still, unarmed, staring steadily. His physical power slowly sapping the Scouser's strength. But a stalemate, nevertheless.

Shaun had one more option. Risky, but he could see the gun man's nerve ebbing away.

Slowly, Shaun swung the bedroom window wide open. In full view, he stood in the sunlight, Irish centred in the gun's scope.

"I'm right here."

His voice carried down onto the ground below.

Startled, Irish moved.

Swinging his shotgun up wildly towards Shaun like he was shooting grouse rising from the moor, he suddenly reared back as Tane Matene threw himself in a death leap onto him.

Triggers were pulled.

The bolt action 0.22 delivered its bullet to the target's head, the hole perfectly centred between his eyes.

Claire screamed.

"Dad!"

On the ground before her lay two bodies.

One dead.

The other, lifeless; the blood seeping from his blasted arm into the sand.

His blown-off hand, fingers curled, lay discarded a few feet away at the water's edge.

EPILOGUE

--------*--------

"Nau mai, Haere mai."

The still air is filled with the strong, powerful Karanga call from the small black-lipped lady in front of the red-carved marae. She invites the guests to step forward into the holy meeting house of her ancestors.

Surrounded by my new family, I smile nervously at my koroua and kuia. My grandparents. They're so lovely. I've stayed with them quite often, and I love to spend time cooking with my kuia. And she's made a special manuka honey balm for my scar. It's helped a little but I'm not fooling myself, the scar is with me forever. I've made my peace with it.

Kuia calls me, 'Her lost one'. Her two daughters, Amiria and Areta, my aunties, are much younger than Tane and Ari. They stand beside her now and I can tell that she's proud of them. A doctor and a lawyer.

Ari stands alongside Shaun. And towering over me, at my other side is my father, ex-gang leader, Tane Matene.

I place my hand on the crook of his handless arm. I can tell that it's a big day for him too.

The crowd squashes into the marae and there are too many people for me to spot faces. It's a big blur, but I know that Frank and Celia are in there somewhere.

It was touch and go if Frank would make it at one point, he'd lost so much blood. Physically, he's recovering well. But, he's not been back into the store, even though it's been over a year. They've been travelling a lot. Italy, France, and they met up with Christos in Crete.

A manager's running the camping shop until it's sold. Frank says he'll not miss it, one jot. Plus, it means he has more time teaching Shaun and our lake lodge visitors how to fish like a Kiwi.

"Dad?" I whisper in Tane's ear. "We've been wanting to ask you something?"

Shaun and I've been discussing this, and we really want to do it. Now seems the right time.

"Can we take your name? Cobain means nothing. Your family are everything to us."

The big man breathes heavily, kisses me on the cheek and gives a nod of consent to Shaun.

"I'd be honoured," he says. "I thank God every day that you found me."

My heart fills my chest. All the things Tane has been and has become. Professional athlete, hard-nut criminal, an amputee. And now, after six months of training, an inspirational speaker. He's been going around schools talking about life choices. I am deeply proud to call him my dad. When I used to think about his name on my birth certificate, fantasise about who my father was, I never imagined this.

Shaun squeezes my hand.

"You look so beautiful, Claire."

And a little bewildered by the words in this strange language before we step up to take our vows.

"We've got this," Shaun says softly to me, feeling my nerves.

We place kākahu, capes of feathers, around each other's shoulders and come together in a hongi, our noses touching in exquisite silence. Man and wife.

There are no rings. Instead, two matching intricate designs swirled in black lie over our ring fingers, pointing upwards across the back of our hands towards our hearts. Our commitment etched indelibly onto our skin.

After the ceremony, the guests line up and press their noses to ours, welcoming us into the family.

Later, there'll be more. Much more, with singing and dancing, hakas and hāngi; traditional Māori celebrations.

The line of family finally dwindles.

"Mr Matene," I say with a grin, gazing up into his deep blue eyes, our first moment alone.

"Mrs Matene."

He leans down, his lips meeting mine, then kissing me deeply.

"Uh-hum!"

Somewhere a throat is cleared very loudly.

"Err...sorry to interrupt." The voice is British and male.

We pull apart.

"We weren't sure what to do about the noses thing."

"Oh my God! Annie. Jac. Jason..."

"And this is Luke," Jason adds.

"Luke. Great to meet you."

Shaun embraces Jason's partner.

"You're here!"

I hug each of our friends in turn.

"But...How? I thought you couldn't come... and where's little Seren?"

"Callista's got her," Annie grins, "No way could we miss this."

"And you've been here the whole time?"

Annie nods.

"We were at the back, in case Seren started joining in."

Callista, Jac's mother, rushes up towards us.

"Claire, my darling. Congratulations!"

She winks at me.

"I knew it wouldn't take you long to find him."

Her long grey dreadlocked hair is held up in a batik print silk scarf, her fine grey linen dress hugging her slender, willowy body.

I can't help myself, I snuggle Annie and Jac's baby girl in my arms.

"She's so adorable."

"Who's that?"

Callista's eyes wander towards the tall tattooed man standing across from them on the other side of the marae.

"Callista, let me introduce you."

Taking her breath away, Tane Matene leans down, a little shyly if I'm not mistaken and presses his nose to hers. They move apart but their eyes are still on each other.

The look I give Annie makes her giggle.

"What about her partner, Sam?"

I blow a kiss on the baby's cheek.

"Split up a year ago. Too straight-laced."

I can see that. Not everyone can handle Callista's energy and love for life.

It's later that evening when Annie finds me.

Jac has taken Seren to try and get her to sleep, and the party's in full swing.

We've been eating delicious smoked meat and vegetables from the hāngi and there's a big bonfire on the beach in front of the marae.

"I love this place," Annie announces.

I don't disagree. Our new home. My new family.

"You know, there are things I need to tell you, Claire," she begins.

I look at her warily.

"Mum wrote me a letter a few days before she died. Callista gave it to me the day you left on your travels."

"What did it say?"

"Everything about what happened that night my father died. But you know all about that by now, right?"

"Shaun told me about what your mother did. I'm so sorry, Annie."

Annie stares out at the full moon, rising high above the sea.

"She was brave. I don't blame her for what she did. She stood up to him, even though she was dying."

I'm not sure what to say so I stroke her shoulder.

"Shaun covered it up."

A shiver runs through me. Is she angry about that? Does she blame Shaun?

"What've you done with the letter? Did you take it to the police?"

"I burned it. I reckon what's done is done."

Shaun wanders over towards us and takes my hand.

"So, what do you think?"

Annie's eyes meet his.

"I think you did the right thing."

Shaun looks at her confused. Then, I feel him let out a deep breath.

"Thank you for helping Mam."

There's nothing more to say. He lets go of my hand and embraces Annie.

"And what about that?"

Annie signals to me as they move apart.

"What?"

Tane and Callista are still talking together, their heads close as they sit over in a shadowy corner of the dune away from the open bonfire and the other partying guests.

I shrug.

"Old dogs, new tricks."

Annie laughs lightly.

"Good on 'em, I say."

Shaun's arm settles around my waist and he moves his hand gently touching my belly. Because new life is within me too. Still a secret between us and the world, it's no bigger than a thumbnail yet, barely more than a line on a plastic stick.

Shaun whispers, his lips brushing my ear, "And this, Claire, is just the beginning."

BOOKS BY THIS AUTHOR

The Strictly Business Proposal

Freshwater Bay Series Book One

The Actor's Deceit

Freshwater Bay Series Book Two

Their Just Deserts

Freshwater Bay Series Book Three

The Rural Escape

Freshwater Bay Series Book Four

Trust Me

Trust Me Find Me Series Book One

BOOKS IN THIS SERIES

Trust Me Find Me Series

Trust Me - Book One
Find Me - Book Two

Trust Me

A powerful love story with a dark-edged underbelly.

Glyn Evans' death is clearly a tragic suicide. An open and shut case. And yet something about it feels off...

In a single day, Annie Evans' life is blown to bits. It's a huge mess and she desperately needs to escape from London. But that means going home. The place she's been avoiding for years.

Jac Jones is back home too. And Annie's never forgiven him. She vowed to ghost him. Never to see him again. Why didn't her parents know that? Whatever possessed them to let this ex-special forces soldier rent their farm?

Jac Jones is a player. Is he playing her again?

For Sion Edwards, his old army buddy's place is the perfect bolt hole. A safe place to hide from the people who want to make him pay for what he's done.

And they won't rest until he's dead.

The detective is right. In this sleepy Welsh valley, not every-thing is as it seems…

An addictive and compelling exploration of trust and betrayal.

PRAISE FOR AUTHOR

Reviews of The Freshwater Bay Series

The Strictly Business Proposal
The Actor's Deceit
Their Just Deserts
The Rural Escape

'*Highly recommend the whole series. Brilliant characters, with interesting and exciting plots. Beautifully set in Wales.*'

'*You won't be disappointed. A most enjoyable read.*'

'*Really enjoying this great series, Freshwater Bay. Each book keeps you captivated, not wanting to put it down.*'

'*Ok, somebody just transport me to this beautiful picturesque location in Wales. Such fun and delightful read!*'

'*Well written believable characters, good storyline and pleasant settings craftily described. I could see the places and buildings and feel the air. Nicely done.*'

ABOUT NELL

Sign up to Nell Grey's newsletter for news about Nell's novels and access to some great book offers

Follow Nell Grey's Facebook page and never miss a story.

https://www.instagram.com/nellgreybooks/

https://twitter.com/NellGrey1

https://www.goodreads.com/author/show/19699050.Nell_Grey

Printed in Great Britain
by Amazon

69005048R00142